DRACULA
BEYOND STOKER

Issue 4

DBS Press

Dracula Beyond Stoker
Issue 4

Tucker Christine
editor

Edward G. Pettit
Shannon Vare Christine
consulting editors

Published by DBS Press
ISBN - 978-1-963391-02-2 (Paperback)
ISBN - 978-1-963391-03-9 (e-book)
May, 2024

www.dbspress.com
www.draculabeyondstoker.com

Contents

30 April

My Dearest Reader,

More than any other characters in *Dracula*, including Renfield and even the Count himself, the Brides remain a profound mystery. They lack a backstory, defining traits, and are not even granted names (more on that shortly). In fact, the term "Brides" is a label we as readership have bestowed upon them over the years; Stoker refers to them as "weird sisters" or simply the women, but never as brides or wives.

Yet they hold significance in the novel, in the fandom, in culture, and seemingly to Stoker himself, as they were present from the outset. The earliest dated note in the Rosenbach's collection(March 8, 1890) contains a scribbled outline of Jonathan's stay at the castle and already includes the first appearance of the weird sisters "Young man goes out sees girls one tries to kiss him not on lips but throat Old Count interferes—rage & fury diabolical—This man belongs to me I want him." This scene recurs throughout the notes, becoming one of the novel's most iconic moments.

This issue of Dracula Beyond Stoker is perhaps the most diverse yet. Mark Oxbrow offers a glimpse into the origins of these women, while Erica Ruppert and LL Garland depict their activities while the count was absent. Emily Elledge presents the Sisters Weird in a fairy-tale like narrative, and Jessica Gleason updates us on Drac and Penelope by way of his ex-wives. Jeremy Megargee and Amelia Mangan provide dark, modern interpretations, and Henry Herz and José Panbehchi delve into the noir side.

In 1914, Florence Stoker published a posthumous collection of her husband's work containing the story "Dracula's Guest," which is also featured here. Chris McAuley explores how that story connects to the Brides, while Toothpickings theorizes its possible hidden reference in Universal's 1931 film adaptation.

The issue concludes with not just one poem, but a cycle by Holly Payne-Strange.

Each author had their own method and reasoning for selecting the names they did, and since Stoker provided no guidance, we made an editorial decision not to standardize the names.

This was the most challenging issue to compile to date, but also the most fulfilling. We hope you enjoy it as much as we do.

TUCKER

FRESH BLOOD

White Hellebore, Black Hellebore
By Mark Oxbrow

MACBETH: Witchcraft celebrates
      Pale Hecate's off'rings, and withered murder,
      Alarumed by his sentinel, the wolf,
      Whose howl's his watch,…
      —William Shakespeare, Macbeth: act 2, scene 1

Albin Grau's letter to Professor Arminius Vámbéry,
Buda-Pesth University

Friday 24 April 1903

I pray you will forgive me.

It is done. I have informed Abbot Barbaneagra of my decision. I know you warned me not to act in haste, but I could not, in good conscience, remain.

I fear I will not be missed. I certainly do not think the Abbot was disappointed to see me go!

My treatise is nearly done. But it lacks a title. I am hoping you may lend me your wit. I have nothing but a working title and

I am dissatisfied with it: *A Treatise on the Occult Mysteries of the Black Pilgrimage.*

I intend to publish before the summer is out. I need only write the last chapter: a tale of three vampire sisters near the Borgo Pass, in Transylvania.

Tonight, I depart for the village of Dimitrescu.

Yours,
Albin

Albin Grau: Foreword to Untitled Treatise

You may wonder what it was that ignited my obsession?

Such a strange and seemingly insignificant thing. I bought a ticket to the theatre.

Macbeth. One ticket.Wednesday 24 April 1889. The Lyceum Theatre, London. Henry Irving and Miss Ellen Terry. I had no inkling what it would spark in me.

By the pricking of my thumbs, something wicked this way comes.

There they were, on the stage, upon the blasted heath. The three Weird Sisters. Lit in limelight and cloaked in shadows. And I, in my seat in the upper circle, was enchanted. Bewitched.

In that moment I was a boy again, picking hellebore for my grandmother. Minding its thorns. Sucking blood from my fingers. And my grandmother warning me: 'You must hide your thumbs, or the ghosts will come for you.'

This seemed so absurd. A peasant superstition. I thought nothing of it as a child but now I learn that this belief is over two thousand years old! The Roman poet, Ovid, wrote of this foreboding, and the need to protect yourself by hiding your thumbs. Do we really have a sixth sense? A pricking of the thumbs heralding something uncanny in the air? Ovid knew it in first century Rome before his exile. Shakespeare carried the superstition in 16th century London. And my grandmother believed it in 19th century Transylvania.

My fascination with the lore of superstitions has become, I must confess, an obsession. I have followed dread paths, beset by briars and nettles, to bring these dark traditions to light. My journey has taken me from Scotland to far Constantinople, from the Druidic monument of Stonehenge to the haunted forests of Bavaria, from the lair of the vampire to the necromancer's laboratory.

And so it has been. I have closed the pages of the Bible and devoted myself to the study of the dark arts. The Language of Angels, magic, the Häxan, and the Strigoi. The Hermetic Order of the Golden Dawn, and the Heliopic Brotherhood of Ra.

I can only hope that this treatise will cast light in dark places. An unforgiving light.

A.G.
Wisborg, Germany. April 1903

Journal of Albin Grau

Monday 27 April 1903

I had forgotten. Has it been so many years since I returned to Transylvania?

Endless forests that banish the daylight. Mountains that seem to rise into the heavens. The winter snows have yet to thaw. So close to Walpurgisnacht, but still the winter refuses to die.

I saw a signpost for Zărnești.

My mother, father, sisters, aunts, nieces, so many ancestors, in the town cemetery. No fancy vaults or mausoleums. Wooden coffins. Buried deep in the earth.

I remember the white walls and red tiled roof of the church. Biserica Nașterea Maicii Domnului. Nativity Church. Should I take flowers to my mother? Spill a bottle of țuică on my father's grave. Perhaps.

But after I speak with Ana Florescu. She will tell me of the Weird Sisters of Dimitrescu.

Tuesday 28 April 1903

I arrived after dark in the village of Dimitrescu. The village priest, Valeriu, took me to my lodgings. The village inn has no rooms, so I have a bed in the home of an elderly man, Dionisie Roşu, a former Tischlermeister, a master cabinetmaker. His left eye is blind, white, and he can barely see out of the right. The bed is comfortable and Roşu is hospitable. We drank blueberry afinată until after midnight.

Valeriu arranged my formal introduction to Ana Florescu. We met in the village church. Ana is a quiet woman, a widow, softly spoken and polite. Younger than I thought. She wears an embroidered linen shirt, apron, and skirt, decorated with black crochet lace and hand-sewn flowers. Women, young and old, wear these beautiful clothes across Transylvania. The dresses are usually white with bright petals but, as a widow, Ana Florescu wears black, stitched with deep red barberries, and dark purple hellebore flowers.

Ana Florescu interview, transcribed by Albin Grau,
Tuesday 28 April 1903

'My name is Ana Florescu. My husband was Mihal Florescu, a weaver. My father was Dinu Lazarescu, who kept the water mill. I was raised in the village of Dimitrescu.

It was my mother, Sofia, who told me of the strigoi. We buried my grandfather you see, and I was the child that asked so many questions. Why do we make coliva cake? Why are the mirrors all covered? Why was he buried with coins, and a needle and thread?

My mother told me that the unquiet dead may come from their graves to torment the living. We lit a candle at my grandfather's bedside to light his way to heaven. A mirror could catch his reflection and keep his spirit bound to our home. Every rite must be performed, or they return as a strigoi.

The strigoi are monstrous, the dead that walk. Have you heard of moroi or moroaică? Vampire. The Un-Dead that steal the blood of the living.

My mother remembered her father and her uncles digging up graves in the old cemetery. There were strigoi when she was young. Her cousin was ailing, her skin white and thin. Too weak to rise from her bed. Men took shovels and dug down into the earth. They found the candlemaker fat and bloody in his grave. Blood about his lips and blood pooled within his body. They broke his bones. Cracked open his ribcage and cut out his heart. Oak stakes were driven through his body to keep his corpse from walking.

They burned his heart at the crossroads, near the mountain path. Burned it and made a tincture with the ashes to heal the girl. But she died, three days later.

There were other corpses that had turned in that old cemetery. Villagers dug up a dozen of their kin. Hacked heads from their bodies. Burned their hearts and livers. Hammered rocks into their mouths until their teeth broke. But many villagers died.

It was a winter's night when they saw the vampire.

She was barefoot, wearing nothing but a shift dress. Her hair black. Ravens flew about her. A bird of ill omen.

They saw her where the trees are cut for coppicing, at the edge of the forest, near the mill. And at that moment my grandmother knew her name.

Izabela Lupu.

They were told her story as children. A warning so they would fear the dark. To keep them away from the mountain paths, and the high places, and the castle.

Izabela was the curious child. The one that took to the woods to hunt for berries and herbs. The child with the torn skirt and the lost shoes. She ran from home at sunrise and was never back before nightfall. Until one night she did not come back at all.

The villagers lit torches and searched the forest—half scouring the valley, half following the mountain path. They found Izabela near dawn. She was curled up in a hollow, by the roots of a fallen tree, and a monstrous black wolf lay across her.

Some said it was a wolf, wild, down out of the mountains. Others said it was a ghastly black dog. It stood, arched over the girl, fur bristling. Fangs bared, its eyes burning like coals.

Men circled the wolf, waving torches, shouting, setting leaves and branches alight. The wolf snarled, bounding among the men, scattering them like frightened hens as it vanished into the woods.

Izabela seemed unharmed. The wolf kept her warm that night. Kept bears at bay. But something inside her was changed. A thing that no one could see. It was broken and healed wrong. Her heart still beat but somehow it was dead. All the love she had ever felt or shared had died.

Some say she lost a child next summer. Dreadful, misshapen. A thing of fur and fangs, born dead. They said that she buried it in the forest, by a fallen tree. I do not know the truth of that. The woman that told me that story is a liar. I cannot trust her words.

What I do know is what my mother told me, that Izabela led a young man out to the meadow. He loved her raven-black hair, loved the curve of her soft white skin. She laid him down among the spring flowers and kissed him. Unbuttoned her shirt and danced as she took off her clothes. And she lay across him, took up a horn-handled knife and gouged out his eyes. The knife cut through his neck, and deep into his belly.

An old seamstress saw her that day. Naked, running through the woods, red with blood on her face and her hands, and her body. Saw her run for the mountain path that leads to the castle. To the Borgo Pass, to Castle Dracula.'

Journal of Albin Grau

Tuesday 28 April 1903

Ana Florescu has promised to show me the old cemetery and church tomorrow morning. She tells me that the forest has devoured them, that I will not find them without a guide. I must transcribe the notes of our interview, tonight, before I can sleep.

It seems that the village elders have always told their children tales of the vampire Izabela Lupu. My host, Dionisie Roşu, opened another bottle of blueberry afinată and told me, and the priest Valeriu, that when he was a boy, they called her '*The Countess.*'

She came down from the castle, to hunt in the woods. Izabela ate men's flesh, but she loved the blood of children most of all. He poured another drink.

Wednesday 29 April 1903

I woke at first light.

Today I am to see the places that Ana Florescu described. The old cemetery where her grandfather was buried. The woods where the villagers saw the vampire Izabela Lupu. The crossroads where the strigoi hearts were burned.

The priest Valeriu brought a box of sacred communion wafers, insisting that I take them with me. It was impossible to refuse him.

Ana Florescu interview: transcription and notes by Albin Grau,
Wednesday 29 April 1903

'It is not far to the crossroads. But it is far enough. No one will walk there at night. No one.

That was the candlemaker's house. It belongs to the blacksmith's widow now.

You see that lane, there? That leads down to the meadow.

These young trees. They are coppiced for wood. That is where they saw Izabela.

This way.

Here is the crossroads. Three roads.

That is the mountain path. It leads up to the Borgo Pass, and the castle.

This track will take us to the ruins of the church.

When I was a small girl, Lacramioara Fieraru took her life. I remember her face. So pretty, but always there was a sadness inside her. My brother courted her. Loved her. She was found in the forest with a handful of Belladonna berries and leaves.

The priest would not have her rest in the cemetery. No graves for suicides on holy ground. The priest ordered her body buried at this crossroads. My brother was made to bury her, his beloved. Ordered to take her head with the shovel and burn her heart.'

A.G.: *The crossroads are marked by the stump of a lost signpost. The wood is rotten. It is tangled in ivy and spotted with lichens. The forest was silent there. It is hard to imagine the villagers burying their dead or burning the hearts of their kin in this place. It is peaceful.*

'The old cemetery is a mile or so this way, through the forest.

The trees are older here. The villagers will not cut these trees. We forage these woodlands for herbs and toadstools.

My mother taught me to heal. She made elixirs. We gathered berries, tree moss, mushrooms, and flowers. She would laugh to see us here. My mother loved to laugh and to sing. She would brush out my hair at night and let me brush her hair. Her hair was golden, bright as sunflowers.

You see that? Growing on the side of the oak tree. You boil that moss to make a posset. It is a remedy for consumption. There, that toadstool, blood red, is agarick. It must be grated finely and with bitter apple, black hellebore and Bourdeaux brandy you can make a tincture for purging the body.'

A.G.: *Ana knelt by a fallen tree. She showed me a small plant with dark green, serrated leaves. She told me it blooms with yellow flowers in spring, and fruits with red berries by summer's end. It is the barberry plant, but in Transylvania it is named Dracilă verde.*

'You see it?

That is all that remains of the old church. That tower. When I was little there was a nave here and wooden pews. All the stone is robbed. When the church was abandoned, the villagers tore it down and took the dressed stone for their walls.

If you look there, to the left, you see? That gate post, and a low wall circled the cemetery. It is all gone now. Sometimes the children find skulls here. Tree roots drag the dead from the earth. Hundreds are buried here, but no one will tend their graves.'

A.G.: *I saw white hellebore growing in the ruins of the old church. It was flowering, defying the winter snows. In Transylvania the white hellebore is called 'strigoaie.'*

Ana says that hellebore was used in a potion, to summon the devil. Here the word 'striga' means 'to scream.'

'You have to know why we abandoned this church to the forest.

It was summer. I was nine years old. My mother had a baby in her belly, and my brother had found a new love. Silviea was plain, not like Lacramioara. Her eyes were green, and her hair was nut brown, not black, but she made my brother happy enough.

Silviea made a comely bride, in her newly embroidered clothes, with flowers in her hair.

I remember two candles, there, on the altar, and two Wedding Crowns. It seemed that all the village was there to see the betrothal and marriage. The rings were blessed.

The priest took up a crown.

I remember it all.

My brother smiling, ruddy cheeks, dimples. Silviea so happy. And there, the church door crept open, and she stepped so soft.

I saw the smile fall from my brother's face, heard my mother screaming. It was Lacramioara Fieraru, a dead thing, walking.

Her bare feet were broken at the ankles. Fingernails torn as she clawed her way out of the earth. She walked, half naked, her grave clothes in tatters. Black hair knotted, mouth bloody.

A wolf padded into the church beside her. A wolf, but not a wolf.

I can see it. Huge, midnight black. Fur raised. Paws pad-padding on the wooden floor. I do not know what it was. Do dogs grow so wrong? It bounded over the pews, fangs like knives.

My brother held Silviea tight. He had not cut out his dead love's heart or taken her head. Whether for pity or love, it did not matter. Lacramioara's fingernails cut through Silviea's neck as her teeth tore out my brother's throat.

I felt myself carried up off the floor, saw my father take me and my mother away. I heard the wolf snarling, and the screaming. Bodies falling before us. Torn apart. Eyes staring. The aisle slippery with blood.

My father found a small window. He raised me high, my mother screaming at me to run, to hide. I squeezed through and fell. Broke my finger on the ground. And I ran, with my mother's screaming in my ears.

There was someone sat high on a tree branch. Sat like a crow. Izabela Lupu, like in the stories. Izabela Lupu and her wolf.

I crawled, out there, near the cemetery wall. The priest and some others fled out of the church. But Izabela fell upon them, shrieking. Nails like talons. Hair like raven feathers.

I hid in the woods. Nobody came for me that day, or night.

It was the schoolteacher that found me next morning. The church was burning, with the bodies inside. No gravedigger to bury them. No priest to say words over the dead.'

A.G.: *I scattered some of the communion wafers that the priest Valeriu gave to me in the ruined church. Ana lost most of her family that day. She was raised by her aunt in Podu Dâmboviței, in the Southern Carpathians. Ana did not return to the village of Dimitrescu until 1889. Snow was falling as we walked back to the village, and she talked.*

'I always believed I would come back to Dimitrescu.

My husband, Mihal, was taken by scarlet fever in the winter of 1888. We lost a son, Luca, in his first year. We had a daughter, Sofia, named for my mother. Sofia Luminita Florescu. She had my mother's eyes, blue as the sky, and her hair, it was like spun gold.

She was seven years when I brought her to see Dimitrescu. We would sell what was left, see the winter out, then start over in Bucharest. Sofia wanted to ride in a horse-drawn tram carriage.

It was a harsh winter, dark, with deep snows. Something was wrong with the mountains. Everyone felt it. Doors were barred and windows were shuttered.

It was the Feast Day of Saint Tatiana the martyr. I took Sofia to gather firewood. We did not walk far. She was small and I did not like to be far from home. She helped me find fallen sticks we could dry by the fire and use for kindling.

I only lost sight of her for a moment.

The forest fell silent. I could not hear her singing. There was no crunch of her boots in the snow. Nothing.

I found her footprints near me. They did not stray into the woods. They stopped on the path. I called her name. Screamed it.

It was the Tischlermeister that found me. It was growing dark. He carried me from the forest and his wife gave me liquor as the men began their search.

She was never found.

The villagers whispered that Sofia would be found when the snows thawed. Down in the river.

I waited. Walked the woods and called her name. I waited for winter to end. It was as if the forest had come to life and eaten her whole.

Then I saw them, three sisters, huddled in the treetops. Vampire. Un-Dead.

Blood dripped from Izabela's claws. Blood in the snow. She clutched a dead hare in her hand, gnawing on its throat.

I saw the three, the Weird Sisters. Saw them grinning down at me.

Izabela Lupu. *The Countess.* Dead a hundred years. Lacramioara Fieraru, raised from the crossroads. Their eyes red, hair black as midnight. But the third had hair like gold. Blue eyes. White skin. The third vampire was my mother, Sofia Lazarescu.

She wore some mockery of my mother's smile. This abomination with her face. Took her body as its puppet. Her belly was empty, her dress bloodied. Eyes ice blue.

The three watched me, tearing pieces from the hare. A howl sounded, deep in the forest. It was unnatural, the baying of a Hellhound. The sisters craned their necks, heads juddering. They shrieked and flew from their branches.

Many saw them in those years. Vampires hunted in the forests and in the villages. Three sisters, and Dracula.

The brave and foolish took weapons and the path to the mountains, the Borgo Pass and Castle Dracula. None returned. None until the Netherlander and his English friends.

And so, I stay. There is nothing for me in Bucharest. I will live and die in Dimitrescu, and sleep soundly in my grave.

I have one more story to tell, if you have ears to listen.'

Journal of Albin Grau

Wednesday 29 April 1903

I will meet with Ana Florescu in the morning. She has warned me to wear stout walking boots.

It took many hours to transcribe my notes tonight, but I dared not wait, fearing I may lose some precious detail.

There seems a thread woven through Ana's stories. Some ancient belief that I can see. It is as Shakespeare wrote: *'And now about the cauldron sing.'* Hecate, the Goddess of the Witches, counts the three Weird Sisters as her devotees.

Macbeth: act 3, scene 5 A heath.
{Enter the three Witches meeting Hecate}
First Witch: Why, how now, Hecate! you look angerly.
Hecate: Have I not reason, beldams as you are,
             Saucy and overbold? How did you dare
             To trade and traffic with Macbeth

In riddles and affairs of death;
And I, the mistress of your charms

It is Hecate that is Goddess of the Dead. Goddess of Night and of the Mysteries. She is honoured by the Deathless Gods in Starry Heaven. Hecate is the Goddess of the Crossroads, worshipped at the meeting of three roads.

Hecate is the protectoress of dogs, she who haunts the mountains. Black dogs are sacred to her. If Hecate is near, you will hear the barking of the dogs of the underworld.

The Goddess Hecate has three faces, three heads, three bodies.

Is this not akin to the three vampires? Their wolf or spectral dog. The crossroads and the dead.

Tomorrow I will meet the widow Ana and have the last piece of this tale.

Journal of Albin Grau

Thursday 30 April 1903,
Walpurgisnacht

Dionisie Roşu, woke me close to dawn.

He clattered about the kitchen. Gathering pots and sharpening a knife with a whetstone.

I asked Roşu what made him wake so early. He told me he will go to the forest to gather the *Armindenul*. Green branches to hang above his door tomorrow. The first of May is Wormwood Day. Greenery protects the home and the stable.

This night, in Germany, it is Walpurgisnacht. They say that all the witches meet on the Brocken Mountain, to dance as winter wanes.

I asked Roşu if he knew of 'the Netherlander and his English friends' that Ana spoke of. He did more than remember. He has a photograph. Roşu told me proudly of the camera that he made.

He showed me the albumen photograph, pointing out each in turn.

'That is Professor Van Helsing. Here, you have Mister Harker and his wife, Mina. That man is Holmwood, he is a Lord, and beside him, Doctor Seward. I cannot imagine what they saw. Van Helsing, here, it was he that killed Izabela and her sisters. The others buried a knife in Dracula's heart and cut his throat to the bone.'

'Their friend died at the castle. Mister Morris. I had not made a cabinet in twenty years, but I made a coffin for that man. Oak and rosewood. I could do no more for him.'

I met Ana and we took the mountain path at the crossroads, following it for a little over three miles. Ana tells me that the path to the castle is treacherous in the summer months and all but impassable in winter.

I am indebted to Ana for her advice to wear a pair of stout boots. The mountain rises steeply, and we abandoned the path to follow the river. I did not understand why until I caught my first glimpse of Castle Dracula. There was once a sturdy wooden bridge arching from the mountainside to the castle. That bridge is gone.

Ana says that the villagers burned the bridge. Days after the fall of Dracula and his vampires, the villagers raised the castle, taking anything of value, burning all that remained.

They lived so many years in fear. Now, in some small way, there would be a reckoning. Dracula's castle would fall. Treasures looted, sumptuous dresses, robes and tapestries set alight. Books shredded; their pages thrown on the bonfire.

The ruins of the castle are forbidding. A spike of rock that bursts from the mountains. Blackened towers cling to it. They look, for all the world, like some unholy pagan crown. Not a crown of thorns but of bones. Bones burned and broken.

I wish we could turn back. It is madness to go closer.

We sit by the river, finding a small patch of green. Ana brought bread and goat cheese. She pointed out a dozen herbs that grow by the river. This is a secret path. Ana's mother took her here to pick white and black hellebore.

Journal of Albin Grau, writing by Ana Florescu

Mr. Grau has fallen and injured his wrist.

The path to the castle is perilous. It is little more than a narrow goat track and he caught his foot on rocks and ice. I do not think his wrist is broken but he has wrenched it. His fingers are swollen and sore to the touch. Mr. Grau has asked if I will write notes in his journal.

He finds the ruins of Castle Dracula quite overwhelming. 'Monstrous' is the word. 'Spires like blackened oak stakes. Iron jaws for gates.'

Every stained-glass window is smashed, every painting slashed to pieces. The smaller furniture: chairs and tables have been robbed out. Larger furnishings were dragged out to the courtyard, to the flames.

Mr. Grau prodded and kicked over the bones of the bonfire with his boot. He was particularly upset to find tatters of parchment pages and the spines of books among the embers.

Birds roost in the rafters of the great hall. The fires tore a hole through the roof. Rain pours in but it has frozen into icicles. There, in the burned black of the hall, these icicles are shining, a chandelier of diamonds.

We descended. Mr. Grau wanted to see where the three sisters met their fate.

The way is fraught. The cellars and crypts are carved from the rock, beneath the castle. Spiral staircases are broken, treacherous.

Their tombs lie in a chapel.

It is a vault, with carved pillars and arches of stone. The villagers unleashed their fury on the tombs, breaking one to pieces. Mr. Grau took time to view the tombs in turn, closely examining each by lantern light. Among the ruins is soil, and ashes, and small fragments of bone.

Mr. Grau found a piece of jawbone with a tooth intact. It seemed too small to belong to my mother or one of the other sisters. Perhaps it was part of some lost child.

'Voluptuous' was the word Van Helsing used. The Weird Sisters lay on their backs, slumbering in the earth, in their tombs. He was drawn to love them, he told us, protect them, under their spell. But he destroyed them all. Izabela Lupu, Lacramioara Fieraru, and Sofia Lazarescu, my mother.

High, beneath a walled-up window, was the last tomb.

It lies where there was once the altar. The villagers took hammers to the tomb, disfiguring the inscription on its side so it can barely be read: DRACULA.

Mr. Grau scattered communion wafers in the tombs. I did not have the heart to tell him that the rats will eat them.

There was one more thing to show Mr. Grau.

Some worn stone stairs leading down, under the chapel. There is a burial crypt. A hidden chamber with a secret.

Mr. Grau was eager to see. He raised the lantern high. I do not think he expected to see my daughter. Her hair like spun gold. Blue eyes and her skin so pale.

She carried a bundle, cradled it in her arms. Mr. Grau screamed when he saw the baby. My mother's baby. Born Un-Dead, cut from her womb. She is my sister.

I cracked Mr. Grau's skull with a rock.

Dragged him closer and broke his bones. Broke both ankles, and shinbones, wrists and hands, arms near the elbows. Broke his jaw so he cannot scream.

My daughter and the baby will feed on Mr. Grau for weeks.

I cut into my flesh, suckling my sister. She sups blood at my breast.

Ana Florescu's letter to Professor Arminius Vámbéry, Buda-Pesth University

Wednesday 23 September 1903

This letter is for you Professor, the one that will read it.

I send you the journal and the treatise manuscript of Mr. Albin Grau, along with an unsent letter. It is the least I can do.

I hope that you will publish Mr. Grau's treatise. He was a kindly man, always respectful, and he fed my family until his death.

You will understand if I do not tell you where I am travelling. Paris, London, Moscow, New York. It does not matter. A widow, her daughter and her baby will attract little attention.

Three lost souls in the crowd. Weird Sisters.

We will feed and grow fat.

Mark Oxbrow is a storyteller, author, and ghost writer. His short story, 'No Doves Come from Raven's Eggs,' was recommended by legendary editor, Ellen Datlow, as one of the best horror short stories of the year in 2019. Truant Pictures (an Animal Logic company) shortlisted Mark's horror screenplay 'She Awakens' for their inaugural genre screenplay competition. Mark's books feature ghost stories, witch goddesses, Arthurian legends, poison gardens, folk horror, medieval monsters, and secret treasures. Over twenty years ago, Mark founded the largest Halloween festival in Scotland.

And You, Their Best Beloved
By Erica Ruppert

The sun sank behind the high mountains, and darkness rose to meet it.

Inside the castle, shadows swallowed the fading light and spread through the ruins that filled the halls. The ruins of tapestries. The ruins of heavy furnishings. The ruins of women who had been beautiful, when they were still only women.

"Amalia," Irinel rasped. "Come away."

In her rags, her yellowed lace, her tattered veiling, Amalia looked lost. Her long fingers picked and picked at the torn seams of her gown with an endless nervous energy. Outside the tall window, the last of the day stained the edge of the dark sky.

"Come away," Irinel said again, wrapping her sharp fingers around Amalia's withered arm. "There is food tonight. Anca brought home a good big girl."

Amalia's pale lips quirked, a ghost of a smile, and she pulled the heavy draperies across the window before she turned away.

"I've an idea, Irinel," she whispered. "Instead of taking the girl for our hunger, why don't we keep her? Raise her. Make her our own."

"Do you still mourn for your children, then?" Anca asked, half-visible in the swarming shadows that folded about her like wings. Her eyes shone softly, like pearls. A moment before she had not been there at all.

Amalia turned away from her sister, her red mouth trembling.

"Must you always be cruel to her?" Irinel chided, steering Amalia into the deeper dark where even the starlight would never find them. Anca glared.

"Come, darling," Irinel said softly in Amalia's ear, just loud enough for Anca to hear her. "You will feel better after you've eaten."

H e has left us here, to starve or not. Again."
Irinel smiled at Anca's complaint.

"But we do not starve. You make sure of it."

"I would rather he did as he should for us. I do not want the risk of it," Anca hissed. "I do not want the risk of any of it. He has gone to seek another place, another conquest, and left us behind again. He has become a fool in his dotage."

Irinel was as quick as a snakebite, tangling her claws in Anca's elaborately knotted hair, her yellow fangs snapping in Anca's face. The grace she wore was gone, and the beast shone through.

"Remember who I am," she spat, her voice like rusted nails pulled from old wood. "Remember what I gave you."

She tossed Anca away from her like a broken toy.

Anca huddled where she fell, her head down, her eyes looking anywhere but at Irinel in her revealed rage.

"Yes, sister," she said to the stones she lay on. "My *Contesă*. Forgive me."

D awn came and the day passed and night came down again.

"Where has Amalia gone?" Irinel asked as she entered the high hall, licking her teeth clean of the stain of her last meal.

Anca threw open the window and leaned out into the dark air, letting it carry her. She floated there, eyes closed, another shadow in the gloom. She breathed deeply, her mouth open, catching a scent on her tongue.

"She is in the forest, wandering among the trees. She does not seem to know where she is going."

Anca let her feet return to the floor, and stood aside as Irinel took her turn.

After a long look into the black valley, she turned away.

"I think she does know," Irinel said. "Now, go get us something to fresh to eat."

Amalia returned after midnight in a cloud of dust and shadow, nodding silently to Irinel as she entered the hall. Irinel gestured for Amalia to sit beside her at the worm-eaten wooden table. Amalia sat at the edge of her chair, eyes down, plucking at her torn sleeve, pulling threads from the ancient lace. Irinel watched her, a subtle smile on her lips, silent.

When Anca reappeared she carried a lamb with her, half-grown and crying for its mother. She pet it to quiet it, scratching its ears with her sharp nails, careful not to break the skin.

"You're lucky this was easy," she said, holding the animal before Irinel. "I do not like to hunt so hungry. It leads to mistakes. Like that time we took the *pârgar*'s son. He set the town on us to get the boy back. Remember, Amalia?"

Amalia looked at her sister, uncertain, knowing a trap had been sprung but not knowing what it was. Under her nervous fingers her sleeve tore to shreds.

"Enough, Anca. You are always so ugly. You know she was not with us then," Irinel said.

Anca bowed her head, but she kept her eyes on Amalia. When Amalia noticed, Anca slowly smiled.

First Irinel drank from the lamb, delicate despite the ragged gash she tore through the beast's wooly coat. Then Anca had her fill, and handed the weak, bleating thing to Amalia. Amalia bit deeply into the lamb's neck, gulping down the slowing blood as it pulsed from the wound her mouth made. When the animal lay dead she pushed it away and stood, brushing her skirts straight and sucking her long teeth. Her white cheeks held a faint, borrowed bloom.

"When he comes back he will see that I am still the one he chose."

Anca laughed, the sound like a racking cough.

"He will not come back for you," she said, wiping a dribble of blood from her chin. "He barely remembers us, I think. He will come back for himself, and nothing else."

She turned to Irinel. "I will provide for us until he does come back. But we must look further than the nearest village, or even the next, or the rabble will grow brave enough that we will draw our own doom down upon us."

"You forget yourself. Again," Irinel said, her voice poisonous and soft as a feather. "They have not been so brave, yet, that we need to consider them a threat."

Anca glared at her sister, yellow light in her eyes.

"No, not yet," she said. "But their mood is growing bolder. You do not go out enough to see it, not among them, but they do not fear the dark the same way they did when we were young and wild. A boy chased me tonight, with a torch in his hand and a silver cross."

Amalia twitched at Anca's words, but Irinel only waved her narrow hand, dragging darkness through the air like a vapor.

"We have survived worse than silver," she said. "We will again."

The next night Irinel made Anca wait with her, holding court at the bloodstained table while Amalia was gone again into the blackness below. Anca paced.

Irinel smiled when Amalia swept up the long staircase and into the hall, clutching a white-wrapped bundle almost as tall as she was.

"Ah," sighed Irinel. "You have found one who suits."

Amalia faltered, uncertain, as she came forward to show them what she held.

A girl whimpered wordlessly in Amalia's thin, strong arms, her threadbare nightdress no barrier to the stagnant cold of Amalia's breast.

"So, you do know how to hunt," Anca said. Her narrow face twisted with mocking amusement.

Irinel stood and moved to be between them. The girl looked at her for a moment with pleading eyes, until she recognized that Irinel was just as cold as what held her.

Irinel stroked the girl's face gently, following the warm curve of her cheek as she shrank away.

"A pretty thing," she said, her long canines dimpling her lip.

The girl sobbed, and Amalia held her more tightly.

"Come, now," Anca said. "I'm hungry. Let us eat."

"No," Amalia growled, suddenly all claws and sharp fangs. The girl screamed at her ferocity, a child with its night terrors come to life. "She is mine. Go get us another, if you want to eat it."

Anca fell back and glanced at Irinel, then smiled slowly, her jaws as long as a wolf's.

"All right, little mother. This time, all right."

And she was gone out into the dark.

Irinel coaxed Amalia's grip on the girl to loosen, then took the child from her arms.

"She is a nice one," she said. "You did well."

She dipped her head and nicked the girl's ear with the tips of her teeth, enough to get a small taste of blood. The child flinched. Irinel kissed her forehead, and handed her back into Amalia's keeping.

"You did very well, my dear. Be careful of her."

She is bound to me, now," Amalia said, stroking the girl's long braids. "She will not tell me her name. So Instelata, we shall call her."

The girl stood silently as they talked around her, her eyes darting from one to the other while the three sisters spoke.

"I don't think she understands us," Irinel said, watching the girl's confusion. "Or at least not well. Our words have changed their meanings over the years."

Anca smiled, her tongue lolling like a wolf's.

"*Am să te mănânc, micuțule*," she said around her wet teeth.

The girl shrank away. Anca laughed.

"She understood that," she said.

Amalia cringed back, pulling the girl to her.

"So, little one, if not you, then who?" Anca teased, reaching for her with clawed hands.

Amalia threw the girl down and flew at Anca in a rage, her form changing into something all angles and daggered fangs as she caught her sister in her bony arms and bit deep into her face.

Before she could rip free a mouthful of Anca's bloodless flesh Irinel, a black mist in the air, forced them apart. Amalia howled her despair. Anca cowered before Irinel, her torn face already knitting back into its human shape.

"Amalia," Irinel said, calm, too calm. "This is a game you play. That is all it is."

"She will not threaten my girl, not while I stand," Amalia cried, something like human pain in her voice.

Irinel raised her long hand in warning. Darkness webbed her fingers, trailed from her claws like gauze.

"You may have your toy. Do not expect it to be more than that."

Irinel turned.

"Anca, leave them alone," she said. "It will not last."

D ays faded. Nights swelled. Amalia kept the girl with her like a poppet, coddled and fed with raw meat and drops of blood.

T here are men at the gates, Irinel," Anca said. Her teeth grew longer on the words. "They are waiting for morning to come."

Irinel paused at the edge of her carved stone coffin. She looked back at the wide black space of the cellar, toward the stairs leading up to the main level of the castle. After a moment she sighed.

"Calm yourself," she said. "The gates will hold."

Anca snarled.

"Until they do not," she spat. "Who is the girl Amalia stole? Who is she, that there are men at the gates?"

Irinel sighed again.

"Does it matter? They want her back, is all of it."

Anca took a few hurried steps toward the stairs as the dull sound of wood on stone sounded from outside.

"The gates will hold," Irinel said, and lay herself down in her grave.

Anca turned back, muttering an old curse, and joined her.

T he girl moved her mouth around her small new teeth, restless and uncomfortable. Amalia had misjudged how far she had taken her, how much of the stain was in her now. It wouldn't matter, soon.

She picked through the decaying heaps of finery and jewels that had been amassed over the years, searching for something that would turn her Instelata from a pretty girl to a beauty.

"Here," Amalia said at last, gathering a swath of brittle fabric and a handful of jewels. "Stay still, now. Let me work."

When Amalia was done dressing Instelata she stepped back, held the girl's shoulders, and gently turned her to admire her from different angles. The girl was lovely in the dusk, draped in cloth of dulled gold, her dark hair laced with pearls and ruby beads that shone softly in the fading light.

Anca resolved from the shadowy hall. "She looks like you did, before."

Amalia started. She touched her own cheek, her own throat. "Does she?"

"Yes. Perhaps she is a descendent. Our families never did leave these mountains."

Amalia looked at Anca, a different hunger in her eyes.

"She is like a new version of you. Like you are beginning here again," Anca said, her voice a rough purr. Amalia listened.

"I wonder what he will think, when he sees her," Anca said. She curled her arms around Amalia, drawing her close.

"I wonder if he will remember you," she breathed into Amalia's ear.

Instelata stood at the tall window as the bright line of dawn cut the horizon. Amalia rested her long hands on her shoulders. She let herself see the dark mass of the mountains through Instelata's eyes, and followed the girl's gaze to the faint glimmer of fires far down in the valley below them. The light was as distant and fragile as a spark on the air. It would be erased by the sunrise. The mountains, and Amalia, would still be here.

Anca's words echoed through her memory. Would he remember her? Could he forget her, or any of them?

Nothing would change. The answer would always be just out of reach, the beginning and the end the same moment, always. The sun would rise as it always had, and its long golden rays would find the cracks in the shutters, the gaps in the drapes. Inside the castle the light would split the shadows and make a dull glow around the ruins that filled the halls. The ruins of finery. The ruins of empty rooms. The ruins of women who had been desired, when they were still only women.

Amalia lingered, her mind wrapped around Instelata's without finding a way in. She had never learned the name the girl's parents gave her, or ever heard her speak.

She could not let the girl become one of them. It was only a fancy to be let go. She was only a toy.

Inside her own mind Amalia felt Irinel stretch like a waking cat, reclaiming her as she always did after she had let Amalia taste a measure of freedom.

She had hoped that this time, this time, Irinel would let her go.

But nothing would change.

There were still a few minutes before the rising sun became too strong and drove them back to the sheltering grave. Amalia pressed her icy lips to the girl's hair. Instelata sighed. If they remained here the sun would slice through them like a blade. She would make sure Instelata met it. She would throw her from the high window, to burn as she fell into the consuming daylight. Let the men who had come to the gates catch her, if they could.

She wondered if it were her choice, or Irinel's.

"He will come home, someday," Amalia said to the girl, her voice weak as she tightened her grip, waiting for the light. "And he will remember me then."

Erica Ruppert, HWA, SFWA, lives in northern New Jersey with her husband and too many cats. Her short stories have appeared in magazines including *Vastarien, Lamplight,* and *Nightmare,* on podcasts including *PodCastle,* and in multiple anthologies. Her debut collection, *Imago and Other Transformations,* was released by Trepidatio Publishing in March 2023. When she is not writing, she runs, bakes, and gardens with more enthusiasm than skill.

We, the Daughters of the Night
By LL Garland

I t's been weeks since He left, and for the first time in ages, men have appeared in our woods. They smell of the sea and gunpowder, of foreign lands. The scent pulls and plucks at us even in slumber. We awaken to the promise of a meal—a feast, in fact—our first in so very long. We grew weak, starving ourselves in the hopes of tasting the one He promised us, the one He teased us with, who smelled so deliciously of fear. The skittish, lusting man who somehow got away. We will not let that happen again.

Come, sisters. We feast.

We chase the fading embers of dusk from the castle demesne. Only the stars observe our advance, a moonlit mist coursing through the trees. We pause only to call the pack to join us. There will be enough for all.

Soon, the soft thunder of paws rushes alongside us. The men must hear it too. The wind carries the acrid reek of their alarm.

With a longing howl we greet the wolves, our fellow children of the night. In an instant we transform to become like them— pounding paws, quivering muscle, and questing fangs. Together we run.

The scent is so much keener to our wolf-forms. Smoke and sweat. Unwashed wool and salted meat. Spiced wine and dried tears. The blood tracing through their bodies speeds faster the nearer our pack advances.

Soon, soon.

We ring the clearing where they tremble, our paws mere whispers against the forest floor. Some of us pace while others wait, powerful muscles straining in tense expectation of the moment of action like a cocked shotgun. A dozen sets of golden eyes gaze out from the shadows, joined by our three pairs of red.

They are huddled together, clutching weapons around a campfire. Four men, a boy, and three horses. Two of the beasts are strapped to a cart. They, along with the boy, will make easy enough prey for the younger wolves. The men belong to us.

Sister, it is your turn.

A tall grey wolf steps forward. Her eyes flash white in the firelight. Between one step and the next, her silver-grey fur becomes pale, smooth skin. Pointed ears recede beneath fair waving hair. Crimson eyes flash sapphire blue. Our sister steps out from the veil of trees. A branch snaps beneath her bare foot.

The men startle and spin to face the sudden noise, weapons raised. Their shoulders ease when they realize it's only a woman.

"Puh—please … help me!" She clutches her ripped dress. Heaving freckled skin peeks out of her torn bodice. "Wol—the wolves are chasing me."

Thirsty eyes rake over her. Keen-edged, clinging lust mingles with the sharp scent of fear.

The men eye one another and mutter strange words. They do not speak our language. Our sister makes her effect, nonetheless. They invite her closer, waving toward the fire with puffed-out chests and weapons resting on squared shoulders. Proud faces survey the shadows beyond the tree line. We lurk unseen, our ears low, snouts close to the ground, creeping, creeping, drawing the snare tighter.

Not yet.

They offer her food, water, and wine. She takes none. They find excuses to touch her skin. At first, they reach out tentatively, the barest whisper of a finger at her shoulder.

Patience.

Soon their hands become more brazen, as if they believe her body is owed to them for the safety they are providing. Either they do not notice the chill of her skin or attribute it to the cool summer night despite the heat of their flames.

Hold.

Finally, one of the men wraps his rough hand around our sister's wrist. Before he can yank her upright a red wolf strides from the shadows.

No, sister, wait—

In three strides, the wolf leaps, transforming in midair. A dark-haired woman lands on the man's back. Hands clutch his throat. Fangs sink deep. We three sisters fall upon the man.

Blood, blood our only thought, thrumming with each beat of his dying heart. We feast until only a rigid husk remains.

The flavor of lust lingers on our lips, stinging and cloyingly thick. His greed—cold, sour, and weak—stains the backs of our fangs. But it is the burning sensation, clinging to our throats, that draws our attention—spicy and urgent, fiery with delicate sweetness.

What is this, sisters? It tastes so much … richer. Deeper.

This is what He kept from us, feeding us only children who knew nothing of such things.

More.

We drop the spent body and turn on the other men, greeting our meal with courteous smiles. We dance and lick the blood from our dripping fangs. Firelight glints off their widening eyes, yet still we scent lust in the air. Our laughter breaks the spell and the men run.

The youngest wolves pounce on the tethered horses and the boy quivering beneath the cart. The rest of the pack gives chase.

We transform in an instant, and with a howl, we join in the hunt.

They're chasing the men away from the castle.

We need to make them turn around.

It tastes better when they run.

We circle the pack. The grey and brown wolves nip at haunches and shoulder our brethren, while the red wolf runs in a yapping loop, trying to steer them up the hill toward home. But the pack will not be turned. It is as if the trees themselves call to the wolves.

The prey staggers and falters on the rocky terrain. Snarling wolves close in. One of the men glances over his shoulder and shouts something to the others before they run, slipping between bared teeth and snapping jaws. But the wolves do not attempt to snare them. They let the men flee beneath the dense canopy of the oldest part of the forest.

They're getting away.

No, sister.

Wait—

The red wolf plunges in and is swallowed by the trees. The grey and brown wolves trail after her.

The pack waits, a line of golden eyes glinting from the edge of the ancient copse.

Soon, the trees grow so dense we must weave between and around them as mist. How were the men able to make it this far in the tangle of branches and trunks? Still we chase, coaxed by the intoxicating reek of fear.

Cliffside trees bowing with sun-laden fruit.

Seaside terraces…

…where even the air sang with their clear, sharp scent.

To us, the taste of fear is all too common. It is also our favorite. One of us tasted the yellow fruit once, lifetimes ago, but our memories have become so twisted and gnarled we no longer recall which sister it was. We cling to the memory. For centuries now, the taste of fear in our prey's blood is as near as we've ever approached to the gentle warmth of sunlight caressing our shoulders.

Look—

There.

In a small clearing, three men struggle, lashed to three tree trunks. Shafts of moonlight stroke the roots and vines binding their ankles, wrists, and knees. We do not stop to question this strange grove. Thrumming veins at the men's throats call to us. We do not resist.

We regain our true forms and leap at their throats, plunging our fangs deep. It's only as we tear into them that we notice the men's muffled screams. Bark grows over their faces, muzzling their mouths, and spreads across their faces until only their wide rolling eyes remain visible. Soon, even the eyes stop moving as we drink our fill.

"Just look at yourselves…"

A withered old woman stands in the clearing. Dirty shawls do nothing to hide her spindly frame. A threadbare dress reveals knobby, stubbly knees and bare, mud-crusted feet. Bedraggled white braids cascade over her shoulders to puddle on the ground, collecting leaf mold and dirt. The polished jade necklace hanging from her neck is the only item untouched by the filth of time.

How dare…

Who does she think she is?

Perhaps dessert.

Our muscles tense, preparing to pounce on the shriveled morsel. Instead, at a simple gesture of the hag's hand, the trees converge. Twining branches hold us fast. Roots and vines weave, cleaving us to the trunks and the bodies of our victims. We struggle against the forest slowly creeping over us. Devouring us. We cannot change form. Cannot escape.

"Pitiful creatures…" The woman's thin lips twist in a sneer. "Captive to your desires and the desires of men."

Call the pack.

Watch them rip the witch apart.

"Aaa-roooooo. Oooo."

Even our keen ears don't detect their approach until they're padding into the glade, heads low and ears back. The largest wolf stalks toward the old woman. It won't be long now. Rather than spring at her throat, he sits back on his haunches and leans against her leg, a low rumble strums in his chest. Gnarled fingers, like fallen twigs, scratch between his ears. The others wag their tails lazily. Jaws droop and tongues loll.

We snarl at the faithless beasts.

Traitors.

Has she compelled our pack to do her bidding?

We must hurry. Dawn approaches.

"Please, old mother, let us go," one of us pleads. "It is getting late. We must get home."

"Tsk, tsk. The innocent act won't fool me. I know what you are. And I will teach you greedy children patience."

As she curls her hand into a fist, the glade rings with thunderous cracks. The trees at our backs peel apart, layer by layer until the heartwood itself splits, gaping wide. Branches push and vines pull, dragging us toward each tree's center. Something slips at our backs, and we shortly find roots clawing away at the ground. A pit, reeking of damp earth and decay opens at our feet. More roots drag the corpses of our victims into the dirt before smoothing over the grave as if it had never been there. Meanwhile, each tree slowly closes over us, sealing us inside. The wood holds us fast, pressing our arms, crushing our chests, until the only sound is the sparse drumming of our pulses against unyielding timber. The scent of our own fear engulfs us.

Bark stitches itself over the rend, like a scar marking a healed wound. Only our faces remain free of the wood's grasp.

"Set us free, old woman."

"… and we will let you live in peace."

"The Count will come looking for us and he will not be so kind."

The witch laughs. A sound like wind rustling dry leaves. "I have roamed these woods far longer than any of you, longer than even your Count. I know everything that comes and goes in this forest. I know he has abandoned you. I know you hunt each night, feeding on hares and geese like ravenous beasts. Uncontrolled. A plague on this land. For too long I've neglected my duty to these woods. No longer."

The woman finishes her speech with a resigned nod. The trees press in on us further. Wood creeps into our vision, crawling across our cheeks and climbing our chins. We hurl threats and curses at the woman. We hiss and bare our teeth.

"Go on and snap your little fangs," the Forest Mother says as the wood knits itself shut over our faces. "I have tamed worse than you."

It's impossible to say how long we've languished, trapped within the witch's glade.

During the day, the trees shelter us from the sun and allow us to slumber. The old woman keeps us fed, although where she gets the blood, we'll never know. It tastes earthy, fortifying, and warm, like the hazy memory of a stolen crust of fresh sweet bread and familiar tales beside the oven. It clings, thick and sluggish on our tongues.

At night the wood peels away, and she speaks to us; sometimes one on one, sometimes to all three of us. We don't bother listening to our captor, we have each other.

What does she want from us?

Why hasn't she killed us?

She talks too much. Perhaps she's lonely.

Don't listen to her words. She's trying to enchant us.

Wriggle a hand free, sisters. If we can reach our faces, we'll hold the wood open then escape and kill her.

She may be a witch, but she is wise. Perhaps she'll help us. Do you really want to be as we are forever?

After what seems like weeks, a new sensation intrudes in our thoughts. A vivid, searing pinpoint of panic, hunger, and want pulses nightly in our minds. He has created another sister. We reach out to her, to calm her and perhaps seek her help, but soon her voice falls quiet, almost as quickly as it had joined us. Yet His remains, a steady blue wisp in the background of our minds, always lurking, distant and cold.

Worse still, a distance grows between us sisters. Subtle changes arise, even as we retread old arguments.

What's so wrong with how we are?

We should kill her.

I don't want to live like an animal—governed by instinct and need. I could be more.

What do you mean, "I"?

I *should kill her.*

Fine … we could be so much more.

One night, the old woman kneels beside my tree, scraping away the soil with her bare hands and planting bulbs of garlic. I am surprised to find I was not repulsed by the smell.

"It is a shame what he has done to you children," she says, shaking her head. Her braids ripple in waves.

"You are a fool, mother. He made us strong, stronger even than you."

She scoffs, sitting back on her heels. "You girls are root-bound. Your minds are so twisted up together, you cannot tell your own thoughts, emotions, or pasts from your sisters'. Can you even remember your own name?"

Unbidden, my mind swirls with a flurry of images. Glimpses of a forgotten life. I have no interest in them. Not anymore. "We have no use for names. We are so much more now."

She stands and wipes the black dirt from her hands on the front of her dress. "Until you learn to untangle yourselves and root in new soil, you will never flourish."

Later, I call out to my sisters, eager to mock the old woman's words. My own voice echoes flat in my skull. I am alone with my tangle of memories.

The woods witch has won.

Our eldest sister, His favorite, stands beside the witch one midnight, free of her tree. Her hands are clasped tightly at her sides.

"I am leaving, sisters."

What? You can't…

Visions flood my mind: A candlelit ball room … A fair-skinned girl in a fine beryl gown … A handsome dark-haired suitor with a strange accent and knowing smile … A violent kiss on a terrace surrounded by the yellow fear-fruits…

"Lemons," she whispers. "They're called *limoni* in my language. I remember now."

Was that when it happened? When he claimed you?

"Yes," she glances down at her feet, unwilling to meet our glistening eyes. "I want to see my home again."

No. You can't leave. We are one. Undivided. A pack.

The heartwood resounds with the tremors of my captive body. An invisible hand clenches my throat and tears stream down my face. It has been decades since I've cried. I foolishly believed I'd forgotten how.

"I am sorry, sister. This life was never my choice."

Her lips brush gently across my cheek, then she is gone.

Eventually, my younger sister breaks the silence of the glade. I was so swaddled in my own shock, nursing my rage and hurt, I hadn't noticed her conspicuous calm.

"I wish to leave, too."

Why? There's no one waiting for you. No friends, no family. They are all gone long ago. I am all you have left. Why would you go?

She won't respond, won't even glance in my direction.

Sister, please … Don't leave me.

"Don't be so dramatic. We aren't really sisters. We were never anything more to each other than His victims."

"If this is what you wish…" When my sister nods, the witch waves a hand and the tree splits. My sister steps out, takes a few stumbling steps, then sprints from the glade without a backwards glance.

I call them through our connection until dawn threatens. My cries echo back to me empty and unheard.

"And what about you, child. Do you believe you're ready to move on?"

I glare at the smiling old woman. "There is nothing left for me out there."

Nights bleed together. The witch allows me to come and go from my tree as I please, but I have no impulse to stray far. She talks to me for hours. I shut my eyes and ears to her. I wish I could shut my brain to the unrelenting onslaught of my own memories. They wash over me in waves now that my sisters and their thoughts aren't here to support me, to drown out the truth I don't want to remember.

Glimpses of the man I once loved … The simple home we shared … My husband walking away with the other men, his grandfather's sword strapped across his back … The strange, foreign man who visited my starving village, his pockets filled with gold, pleading for a room … The women who cared for me in my illness, then cared for my child after they buried me … My baby daughter. My first victim … I can still taste the cloying sweetness of her blood … The women hurling their stones and curses … The burn of their crosses.

When I refuse to eat, the witch commands branches to pry my mouth open and places her own bleeding fingers on my tongue.

I need your help, witch."

The words taste bitter in my mouth. For weeks now I've said nothing to the old woman about the new visions intruding on my purgatory, growing stronger, more insistent with each passing night. At first, I am grateful for the dark, oppressive gloom numbing my memories. Then I realize what it must mean: He is coming. And He brings a new sister. She burns in my mind like a hearth fire—warm and gentle, welcoming. No … she's not quite a sister. Not yet. This girl is strong. She resists Him, resists the call in her blood—the hunger—in ways I never could. The girl travels with a group of hunters at her side. Her hatred and fear of Him call to me, resonating with my own. I will do what I can to ensure these hunters are successful.

The old woman doesn't answer for a long while. Instead, she continues mending the cracked horn of a viper coiled in her lap.

Eventually, the snake slithers away and she sets aside her pot of foul-smelling unguent. "What is it you need, my child?"

"The Count returns. I need to know how to kill him." When she remains silent, I add, "It's the least you could do after stealing my sisters from me."

"What makes you think you need my help?"

"Even with my sisters we couldn't harm Him. Every time we tried, we failed. And the penalty was steep. But alone … it is impossible."

"Don't be a fool. How do you think the Count is able to act for himself? To plan, to prepare, hmm? He's no different than you in his needs and his thirst. But he is able to harness that drive and turn it to his purpose. And who do you think taught him to do it?"

I look more closely at the withered old woman. Her arms and legs are strong despite their diminished appearance. Eyes shine a little too bright. And her blood—it wasn't thin and weak like other elderly people's I've tasted. Rather it was robust and vigorous, the sap of a strong tree.

"Just how old are you, mother?"

She brushes her fingers against a moss-covered trunk and smiles. Her teeth are strong and sharp. "Old enough, my dear. Old enough."

"So, will you help me?"

"My duty lies in protecting this forest. I will do what I must."

We spend the next few weeks preparing for the Count's return. I tell the witch about the hunters chasing Him home; how He fears them despite His power. I do not mention the woman—my almost-sister—who travels with them.

"Perhaps we can find a way to use these men, to turn the Count's fear to our advantage," the old woman says one midnight as we are wandering the woods. She falls quiet, lost in thought, while we locate a stand of blighted pines. I clear out patches of mushrooms blooming at their roots while she digs a channel to divert the pools of standing water.

When the work is done, I ask, "How will manipulating the hunters make any difference? If He finds out I'm helping them, He will hurt me … and you."

"Don't you worry for me, child. You already know how to hypnotize, yes? When you know what it is these men wish to believe, giving it to them is simple."

I awake at dusk and know they are here. My not-yet-sister shines, a beacon in my mind. The gentle lines of her face are as vivid to me as the searing heat of her emotions. I allow them to draw me across the woods, like a moth to a candle. I travel as mist until I find her in a clearing, sitting with a watchful old man. The girl—the man calls her Madam Mina—waits beside a fire. For a long while, I hold back, listening to their conversation and relishing the warmth emanating from Mina.

She is struggling against the hunger. I catch her darting glances at the blue vein pulsing beyond the old man's beard. The craving is so strong it sometimes overwhelms her other thoughts. But she fights it. How has she resisted this long? Perhaps if I hypnotize her and convince her to drain the old man, she will join me. I would have a sister again and share in her thoughts.

Just when the hunger gets to be too much, Mina devotes her thoughts to the men who travel with her. Embracing love. Sharp worry for their safety. Faith in their bond. One man stands above the others in her heart. It's the silly, skittish man who escaped us months ago, but he looks different through her eyes. Her love for him shines with a blinding brilliance.

I am reminded of my own lost love and our poor, dear child. I am certain I once felt this fiercely burning love for them, but the years and His interference have dulled the sharp edges. I allow myself a moment to bathe in bitter regret and mourn our shattered lives. I cannot yet forgive myself, but I never would have done what I did if not for the Count. He took away my choice, made me a monster, bound by hunger, who did the unthinkable.

I won't allow Him to turn this woman into another monster like me.

Swiping a tear from my cheek, I return my attention to the clearing.

Mina's mind tells me what they expect. A trio of giggling, ruby lipped women in clinging silk gowns, their hunger barely contained. Beguiling. Tempting. Threatening.

So that's what I give them. Seeing my sisters again, even though I know they are only an illusion of my own creation, wrenches a mournful cry from my lips. The old man's fear surges. It wafts from him as he paces, brandishing his holy relics at the apparitions. The stinging tang of sunlight.

Limoni, I think, picturing the fragrant, fruited terraces of my lost sister's homeland.

For her part, Mina seems unaffected by my illusions. The battle within herself commands all of her attention.

I carry on, harassing the old hunter until the music of the forest shifts. The creatures of the night grow quiet. Dawn approaches. I've lingered too long. I flee from the clearing, seeking the nearest shelter from daylight—the castle.

I dread returning to my former home, but I am out of options. The sight of the empty stone towers rising above the trees churns my stomach. My knees buckle at the thought of returning to that hated coffin in the bowels of His home. The orange streak painted across the eastern horizon spurs me on.

The old woman waits beside the castle's outer walls, waving me on. When I stumble again, she rushes out, threads her lean arm beneath my shoulders, lifts me to my feet and drags me through the gates. Instead of climbing the steps to the massive door, we turn toward a half-collapsed building leaning against the wall.

"Here, child. You'll be safe in here. I will keep watch." A craggy finger caresses my cheek. "I won't let any harm come to you."

Drifting to sleep amid the rubble of the old groundskeeper's shed, I miss the enveloping scent of living timber.

When I wake the next evening, my head is clearer than it's been for centuries. Whatever Mina and her hunters did, it must've worked. My thoughts are my own. No new sister. No Count. Only my memories. And loneliness.

The scent of freshly spilled blood chokes my senses, calling me from my hiding place. I climb the castle steps. It leads me deeper and deeper until I find myself in the old chapel. I fight the urge to retch at a new, overwhelming stench. Something lingers here. Something that burns my skin and my throat.

It leads me past my sisters' empty coffins. Inside each, a wooden stake stands on end, piercing the wood. I follow the scent further to my own coffin. A filthy, tattered dress is laid out as if waiting for its wearer. A stake is plunged through its bodice, lodged in the wood of the casket's underside. Rich black soil spills from the fabric, resting atop the red-brown dirt of my homeland. A flash of green peeks out from the neckline of the dress. I draw out the old woman's pendant and tuck it in my pocket.

I don't know what happened here. Whatever the witch did … I am free.

A single low, sorrowful cry resounds in the outer courtyard. I rush out to find the pack gathered, facing the chapel, tails and heads hang respectfully low. The leader sits apart and keens his elegy.

Soon, a coarse roar from beyond the castle walls interrupts their solemn vigil. The pack turns, then lopes through the gate and I follow. A beast – no a man – paces beneath the scraggly trees with juddering steps. His skin is charred and peeling. Blood trickles from wounds on his neck and chest.

"You…" A twisted finger points at me. Blistered lips tear in a sneer. "You dare try to keep me from what is mine?"

My throat constricts. It is His voice.

"Did you truly believe some priest-blessed crumbs could keep me from my home?" He gestures to a line of pale morsels ringing the castle walls. I had noticed the same sprinkles throughout the chapel and around the courtyard. If they are communion wafers, how am I able to traverse them?

"Clean it. Now."

His voice is only a coarse rattle, but it envelopes me like a river of molten silver, pressing and burrowing deep in my mind, compelling my legs to move.

I focus, trying to block Him, struggling to control my own body. I am halfway to the Count before I manage to free one hand and squeeze the jade pendant in my pocket.

What would the old witch do? After all I've seen and suffered, I refuse to return to my old ways—beholden to hunger, my very existence at the mercy of His whims—but without my sisters, resistance feels impossible. Even weakened by Mina and her hunters, He is too powerful for me to resist. Why won't He just die?

The pack must sense my panic and desperation. They circle Him, jaws snapping, fur at their shoulders twitching as they prepare to leap. At a sign from the leader, they pounce, tearing at His seared flesh. I growl, spurring them on. The Count fights back with fangs and fists, flinging wolves from Him. But they are relentless.

Without thinking, I call on the trees, gesturing like I've seen the old woman do dozens of times. A nearby oak leans toward the scuffle. One long sharp branch stretches, a dagger aimed at the Count's chest.

Let it be done, I command the oak.

The wood plunges itself through his heart with a crackling squelch. He roars as His body crumbles to dust.

One of the wolves sneezes, scattering His ashes in a cloud. When they settle again, I know He is gone. For good measure I scoop a handful of the crumbled wafer and sprinkle it on His remains. Curiously, the bits only tingle against my bare palm.

The wolves throw back their heads and howl at the moon, and I join them. There is much to do tomorrow night if I am to learn the ways of these woods. Tonight, though, I will celebrate my freedom and mourn my sisters, my lost family, and the Forest Mother.

LL Garland enjoys gaming, writing speculative fiction, and exploring deep, dark woods. She's been called "disturbingly competitive" at all three. She lives in a house with three dogs and two libraries—a fancy one for show, and a hidden one for the weird stuff. You can find more of her stories on her website, llgarland.com.

The Sisters Weird
By Emily Elledge

i. The Weird Sisters

The sisters were referred to as '*weird*,' a term used by peers and elders alike without the courtesy of ensuring their backs were turned. It was an apt description; they were, in every sense of the word, fantastically weird.

Their origins were largely unknown, except that they arrived aboard a shipment of goods to an island near France where there was a seaside town, a church, and little else. It was a night when the warm air was thick with fireflies. As the second to last barge unmoored for the mainland, someone slipped a crate labeled 'oranges' under the lamplight on St. Julian's front steps.

When the nuns opened the slatted lid and brushed away the mildewing straw, they found three infants cuddled together in unseasonable wooly blankets. There was no accompanying note, so the nuns named them Mona, Myrtha, and Mayrina. Nothing, save circumstance, implied they were sisters at all, for the babes were as different from each other in color and size as they were from oranges. Yet, for all their physical differences, as they grew, they became like a single entity with three brains but one mind. They always knew what the others were thinking or feeling, because they thought and felt the same.

From a young age, they'd had a taste for the macabre—or perhaps the macabre had a taste for them. The murder of crows frequenting the cobbled yard delighted in the sisters' table scraps, greeting them shrilly with offerings of their own. They brought trinkets in the glossy crescents of their beaks, dropped them at the sisters' feet, or by the sill at dusk, and collected every manner of treasure. Silver chains, rainbowy pebbles, coin purses, spools of thread. The sisters kept the hoard in a burlap sack under the crooked floorboards.

The Weird sisters spent most of their free time in the church cemetery, by the gray sea, or under the willows. They had a distaste for sunshine but loved to watch the shadows play against the old mausoleum with the spring flowers browning in the grass.

At school, they enjoyed learning with a level of interest beyond typical fascination, in each class except for religion, which they loathed. They'd had their knuckles reshaped from the number of times they fell asleep slumped over their thin, splintery desks, and spent many a hungry night after asking one too many unanswerable questions. All this achieved, however, was a different, more gnawing hunger to develop their own ideas about the world.

All the other children wore customary dark navy or brown frocks without any fuss, but the Weird sisters took to bleaching theirs the lightest white possible with lye, and their solutions worked faster than they should have, so their clothes became the color of sun-washed bones in the warm desert. It made the nuns furious. They only had so much money to run the orphanage, new clothes being particularly hard to come by. They were usually handed down, tailored to fit the children as they grew—which they did little of with such meager meals—and mended at the first sign of wear. At first, the nuns tried to replace the girls' clothes, but those resources were swiftly and verily exhausted, when the sisters simply bleached them, too.

Despite their weird behavior, weird tastes and general aura of weirdness, the Weird sisters managed to straddle the line of nemeses and acquaintances with their peers. Though they didn't indulge in hand games, braid hair, or make friendship bracelets out of reeds, neither did they have bad blood with the other girls. Their male compatriots, on the other hand, held stronger opinions of the Weird sisters. It wasn't just the sisters' propensity to hiss should a boy skirt near their wide berth of personal space, but they also thwarted any attempts at tomfoolery. If a boy snuck into the girl's dorms, the Weird sisters would appear like living shadows peeled from the wall. The moonlight beamed across their thin faces, their wild hair seemed to dance like flames, and their pale clothes clung to their bony arms, so they looked like ghouls with nasty grins. The boys would scramble away like baby pigs, leaving the sisters shaking with laughter in their bellies. Eventually boys stopped visiting the girls' dorms, which was a fine arrangement up until certain things changed and the other girls *wanted* boys to visit, something the sisters found unfathomable. With their interference no longer welcome, they became ugly poltergeists plaguing their peers' love lives. Regardless, the sisters were not lonely. They had each other.

On a brisk, overcast afternoon in their late adolescence, the girls sat in the garden enjoying the weather. Sister Agatha approached with her eyes downcast, hands clasped under her chin.

"Girls," she said. The sisters greeted the nun with indifference, without looking away from their tasks; Mayrina was embroidering silver stars on black linen; Mona had Poe's *Tales of Mystery and Madness* opened flat on her lap; and Myrtha lay in the damp grass on her back, one hand behind her head and the other stroking a crow's silky breast. Sister Agatha centered herself with a breath.

"You're leaving, girls."

"We're finally permitted to find a place of our own?" Mona yawned, turning a page with her long, pointed fingernail.

"I can't wait to sleep in the streets. I've always wondered what it would be like. Do you think we'll make friends with many rats?" Mayrina snipped the thread with her teeth.

"Undoubtedly," said Myrtha, "I can't wait." The crow was nipping lovingly at her finger.

"You've misunderstood, girls. You're finally being adopted! You're to travel at nightfall to the mainland by ferry." Sister Agatha proffered the news with all the excitement of an overzealous vendor, to a heavy fog of stunned silence. Unnerved by the shift in atmosphere, the crow screamed and wildly flapped its wings in the nun's face. She ran away swearing, crossing herself and apologizing to the sky circularly.

"Adopted?" Myrtha balked.

"This will not do," whispered Mayrina, "not at all."

Mona shivered, not from wintertime traveling on the air, but from a marrow chilling sense of foreboding. Suddenly the sisters felt like prey. Stalked, hunted by some unseen and unknown predator. Or perhaps they'd already been caught.

ii. The Weird House

Their new place of residence was a Spanish style castle with a towering, gloomy iron gate, stone gargoyles, and skeletal fruit trees. The woods skirted cliffs sloping into the sea and housed every manner of moss and fungus.

On the first night in their new home, the sisters found themselves seated at the end of a dining table the square footage of the girl's dormitory at St. Julian's. The sisters sat in silence, chairs pushed together so closely their shoulders touched, picking at their food with the tines of their forks. The wait staff watched with near sinister glee, delighted to have young bodies to feed. Conversely, the sisters—who were unused to being cared for— quickly discovered they did not like it. The presence of so many pairs of staring, fearless eyes was an unsettling change. There was also the strange new issue of too much space. Though they had brought their belongings, of which there were few, they wouldn't have needed them; each sister had her own fully furnished room, in her own wing of the castle, with her own lady in waiting. Their closets overflowed with decadent garments in a spectrum of white hues—lace, opal buttons, shoes with heels and black ribbons, glass beads sewn into silk slippers in enough sizes to suit any stage of growth. Dried flowers had been woven together and hung upside down, so the fabrics smelled sweet, and the moths stayed away. They'd never hated anything more. Rather than retire to their individual rooms, they requested they switch with the maids. So the staff luxuriated for the night, then every subsequent night, in the king-sized beds with goose feather pillows beneath weighty duvets. Thick drapes trapped in the warmth of the fireplaces as well as blocking the morning light. The servants slept with such vigor they missed the breakfast bell and woke dazed, well rested, and very late for work.

The sisters shared one of the small beds in the servants' quarters beneath a skylight, which was just a place where the roof had fallen in, and they made a tent out of the bedlinen and piled several quilts over them.

"I can't help but feel we've fallen into a fairytale," Mona whispered.

"You're right," Myrtha replied, "it's the worst thing that could've happened to us."

Mayrina made a small sound somewhere between a whimper and a bitter laugh.

Fairytales, they knew, ended badly. You would be eaten by a hag at best or taken away by a prince at worst. They shared a collective shudder. Something this smooth on the surface must have teeth lurking somewhere in its depths, the sisters were sure of it. But all they could do was wait like geese in the shallows.

iii. The Weird Townsfolk

The sisters quickly grew healthy and fierce. Their minds had never been so sharp as when their bowls were full, and their bones were warm. They had hot baths with cleansing oils each day but still their hair twisted from their heads in gnarls. Regardless, they thrived, living in something akin to freedom that might even be bliss, were it not for the feeling they were like foxes running through the woods, lulled by the apparent safety of the trees while something circles them with deadly intent. Perhaps this was because, though they had nearly spent a full season in the house, they had never once met their adopter. When they asked after him, the servants had little to say except that he was, "Busy. Very,

very busy. Rarely home." He was, apparently, a Count and a trusted royal advisor who spent most of his time overseas in Transylvania. The sisters were told that it was unknown when, or if, they would ever meet him. It was disturbing to think they'd been adopted by someone with no intention of being a parental figure. Why else would someone adopt three girls, they wondered?

"Tax purposes?" Myrtha mused.

"Some public display of philanthropy?" Mayrina countered.

Mona leaned toward the latter but had a sick feeling it was something more nefarious. The sisters tried to keep it from their mind.

While they enjoyed the confines of the estate, they sometimes ventured into town to visit traveling night markets by the marina. They received stares, gasps, ostentatious whispers, the nature of which were either entranced or disturbed. The sisters paid little attention to their effect. They did not go out in frills or corsets—sometimes they didn't even wear stockings—and gentlemen would stare, blushing, a little too long. The Weird sisters were like tempting, cyanide coated apples since they'd finally had a chance to develop, but they greeted their budding womanhood with as much excitement as they did the attention of men—none.

On one trip to the market, while purchasing satchels of herbs, a woman with a ratty face caught her husband eyeing Mona's snowy shoulders. She responded by spitting at Mona's feet and calling her 'witch.' Mona turned a mean eye to the woman, and the bundle of tulips in her arms began to yellow and shrink. The husband watched, horrified, covering the general region of his member with his top hat before dragging their small child away. The woman turned her twitchy pink nose up at them before bounding after her family with the wisps of dead flowers in her arms. Wraith or demon Mona may have accepted, but *witch?*

The sisters didn't revisit the market after that.

Something worse happened, however, one morning while the sisters strolled along the beach. They stopped for a picnic of vegetable hand pies and sherry when a group of schoolchildren gathered and started throwing rocks at them.

"Which one d'ya reckon's gonna be the Count's bride?" crooned a child with a head like a strawberry. It wore a stupid uniform with a yellow bowtie.

"I reckon he's wed all three of 'em," squeaked another with a gap between its front teeth. "Reckon he's bedded them all at the same time, too."

"Ew!" They all squealed.

The sisters looked at each other in puzzlement, ignoring the rocks disappearing into the fluff of their hair and skirts. Till now, they'd heard nothing to indicate they were coming out to society or being courted, curse the thought. They watched seagulls chase the brats away nipping, squawking, and cackling the way gulls do when they're being antagonistic. You know the way.

"What did they mean, 'bride'?" Mayrina tossed a soupy potato to the seagulls.

"It could be townspeople's idea of folklore," Myrtha said, drawing shapes in the sand with a piece of driftwood.

Mona poured another drink into her tiny glass and put the canteen back in the basket. The sherry smelled sharp and was a morbid shade of plum.

"We'll ask after the master of the house tonight to see if there's any meat to the myth. Although those godsdamned maids are tightlipped as ever," Mona swallowed the sherry in one go. It was viscous, bittersweet, and felt warm in her throat. The Weird sisters would sooner die than become anyone's brides, let alone the harem to some old cryptid. They'd show him they would be free, one way or the other.

iv. The Weird Professor

The sisters and the household staff were preparing for the winter solstice. They hung biscuits from the naked limbs of the trees peppering the estate, fixed candles and bows to a fragrant fir inside. They wound red ribbon around every column, insisted the kitchen keep simmer pots on the fire so the place smelled of cloves and fruit peels. They drank a lot of coffee, ate a lot of sweets, and the sisters insisted everyone play charades and wear paper hats. It was the closest thing to a Christmas party any of them had ever had.

Mona scattered seeds by the open windows so birds would warm their wings and eat, when a raven the size of a small cat landed ungracefully in the center of the room. It looked around at all the faces frozen in merriment and bowed, expressing as much embarrassment as a raven can, lowering its scythe-like beak and extending one leathery talon. Mayrina shook it gently with her own hand, as dark as the raven's plumage, and it opened its mouth, the voice erupting from its throat smooth and deep with a strange, heavy accent.

"*I hope this raven finds you well,*" said the voice.

"It's the Master!" cried a maid, who was so excited she had to hold her paper hat to keep it from sliding off her head. A butler began fluffing pillows and checking for dust with his satin gloves.

"*Please, Rudolph, at ease,*" the raven said to the butler, who looked around frantically and turned beet red.

"*Good. Yes,*" the voice carried on as if it were relaying the message in real time. The raven's throat pulsed with effort. "*Happy Yule, one and all, and hearty apologies for my absence. It has come to my attention that we are expecting a visitor. They are, and I cannot stress this enough, to be treated with the utmost care. They should be arriving-*"

Then the double doors flung open, and a man entered with a heroic flourish.

"*Ah. Now, apparently. This is-*"

"Professor Van Helsing, at your service," the man bowed deeply, removing his broad brimmed hat. He wore bottle cap glasses and a suede patchwork trench coat.

The sisters and staff looked back to the raven for an explanation.

"*An old friend and colleague, the professor has come from the Queen's university to take soil samples from the estate.*"

"You make me sound romantic as ever, old friend," the professor laughed. The sisters found his laugh grating, like a jackal.

"Please, pretend I am not here," he waved away a footman trying to replace his hat with a paper one.

"I trust our—well, your—feast awaits you in the dining room. Please eat, drink, be merry! Until we meet again…" Then the raven shut its beak, its eyes went blank, and it began pecking at the birdseed with contented grunts alongside the finches. The party retired to the dining hall where they feasted in tense, one-sided conversation before the sisters withdrew to bed early, leaving their newcomer in the custody of their caretakers.

That night—the longest, coldest night of the year—the moon was full, so bright it swallowed the stars, and nothing stirred beneath it. The whole world seemed to hibernate from somewhere untouched by the glistening snow, in burrows underground, in the confines of hollowed trees or nests under blankets of rotting leaves. The sisters slept, holding each other as usual, as still as the buried save for the soft rise and fall of their warm chests. A figure loomed over them, watching their throats displayed against the backdrop of pillows. The raven's cries cut through their sleep just in time for them to watch the man slit their throats in three swift flashes, so smoothly the sisters had no time to react. As their arteries gushed hot and red, their mouths welled with dark liquid, and their lungs flailed like dying fish, gasping for breath they could not find. The raven flew down from the hole in the roof, descending on their attacker and the man screamed, staggering back. A maid emerged brandishing a frying pan and battered him over the head. More servants flooded around the sisters and covered their wounds desperately with their bare hands. The bleeding did not even slow.

"Please, friends. Allow me," the Count stepped lithely down from the skylight as if he had materialized there. They dispersed, sniffling and smearing their hands on their aprons, while the Count brushed the sisters' hair out of their faces and, one by one, leaned close to their cheeks as if to say goodnight. When he came away, they each had two small holes in their necks. Then something flashed in the moonlight—the assassin's blade—and he held a dripping wrist over each of their slack mouths. Their wounds began to close and shrink into a thin, silver scar stained with drying blood.

"Van Helsing. So, they sent my old friend to clean up the duke's mess at last," the Count approached the unconscious professor, replaced his cracked, bent glasses on the shredded remnants of his nose.

"Daughters?" He turned to the sisters who were opening their bleary eyes. "Enjoy your first meal."

v. The Weird Count

The spread was practically elysian. Cornucopias overflowed with vegetables imported from the Americas and bright lumps of fruit, and a platter held some suckled animal stuffed from the rear. The Count tried to hide his distaste for the smell of the dead creature's blistered, honey basted flesh and instead focused on the aroma of his drink. He swirled his goblet in an air of refinement. The liquid was dark and slow. It smelled like copper pans.

The Count did not care for parties and cared even less for idle banter, but as a royal diplomat it was important to develop rapport with neighboring kingdoms as well as to remind everyone what he was. Give them a chance to feel grateful for his continued symbiosis. The court greeted the Count with a bow, a curtsy, or a kiss on each cold, soft cheek, but could not keep their gaze from flitting to the contents of his goblet. *It could be red wine* they'd tell themselves as they sip flutes of golden bubbly. But if the legends were true, his crystal goblet was filled with something fouler than even the driest merlot. As much as the Count reveled in the pulsing hormones of their fear—the music of their quickening pulses—he could not wait to end this parade of fake niceties and get what he came here for. And he could not get it without first playing these bureaucratic games.

"Do you care for racing, Count Dracula?" asked a French courtier. She exaggerated and warbled her 'r' sounds and fanned herself more quickly, flirtatiously. She had a long, slender neck, so pale you could see the purple webbing of her veins. The Count took a long drink from his goblet.

"I prefer more soothing pastimes, *mademoiselle*," he said with a grin. "Moonlit rides. A sad Russian novel. Poetry, even. My old heart cannot handle the excitement of gambling."

"That is very prudent of you," she said, "but how old can your heart be? You look, how you say, too young to be my father!"

"You flatter me, *mon cher*," he flashed his teeth, "but I am old enough to be your great-grandfather's father."

"*Pardon?*"

"Nothing," he sighed, "return to the dance." She smiled like a sleepwalker and floated back to the ballroom in a daze. She would have no recollection of her conversation with the Count. *Enough of this,* he thought. *I have done my share of partygoing.*

He slipped into the shadow of the empty corridors. His footsteps were silent as he climbed a spiral staircase. He reached the top and there was a room with no door, just an archway, and a tiny window casting a rectangle of firelight from the blazing braziers against the stone floor. There were barrels and crates and old furniture covered in cloths, and the cloths were covered in dust. He waited. And waited. And waited, for what seemed like an eternity, which the Count knew a thing or two about. Then she finally emerged.

"There you are," the Count whispered. His black eyes were soft and glistening. "I waited till I was sure no one would miss me. Come here…"

"Darling," her voice was like the wind, dry, harsh, quiet. "You have to come, *quickly.*"

"Slow down, my dear. We have all the time in the world. It is just you and I…" He pulled her into his embrace but stopped when she resisted against his chest. "What is the matter?"

She looked up at him, her eyes pleading, and tore herself away to pull a lever in the far corner. A trick wall slid open and she led him through a hidden passage to a room with a hatch leading down into the servant's quarters. A bunch of girls were huddled around something in the center of the room, cooing and whispering.

"Leave us!" hissed the woman, and everyone evaporated into their own rooms.

"Lucy," the Count took the woman's hand in both of his, "I thought we might need … a little more solitude."

"This is an emergency," Lucy whispered. "No one else will help me. Please," her gaze would have made the Count's heart skip, were it still beating. How could he say no?

"Tell me what to do."

"Take this," Lucy lifted an orange crate and gingerly placed it into the Count's arms.

"What the hell is this?" he asked, but the Count could smell the contents of the crate and knew it was not citrus.

"Three women have been hanged in the cellar. Servants. They all recently gave birth." Lucy exhaled sharply. She was tired. "These are their babies."

"What am I to do with them?"

"You must take them far away. As far away as you can."

"Why?"

"Can you do it or not?"

"I can, I'm just … Well, I'm confused, my lamb. What are these children to you?"

"I delivered these babies," Lucy patted her nose with the back of her hand. "They cannot be separated, or they wail like banshees. The throne wants them dead, Vlad."

"Why?"

"Why do you think?"

The Count looked at the babes. One was very pale, like a downy swan; one had honey colored skin and eyes like the blue before dawn; and the third was as dark as a trees' bark after a thorough quench of rain.

"My gods," the Count scoffed, "these are the duke's illegitimate children. I smell his blood in their veins."

"I know somewhere they can go, but I need you to accompany them, to ensure they get there safely."

"Lucy…" he looked down into the crate. The babies ogled him with their sightless eyes. The party thrummed below. Lucy's face was sullen but beautiful, and the Count would sooner drive a stake through his own chest than disappoint her. He covered the crate with its lid, scooped Lucy up with one arm into a deep, hard kiss, and left without another word. He flew back through the hatch and the passage, down the spiral staircase, impossibly fast and quiet. As he left the party carrying the orange crate, no one questioned the Count. They were all too terrified of becoming the next person to fill his goblet.

That was seventeen years ago.

vi. The Weird Family

"Where is Lucy now?" asked Mayrina, wiping the scarlet from her lips.

"She died some time ago," said the Count, "but she would be glad to know I have finally settled down."

"I suppose we owe you thanks for not draining our blood when we were infants," said Myrtha.

The Count wrinkled his nose. "Disgusting. Blood must ripen —it gets better with age. Sweeter. Human babies are like … small animals to me. Very cute, but equally disgusting."

"What about the rumor circulating town? That we were to be your brides."

"Ech! Humans really are perverse," the Count shuddered and took a nip from a flask he materialized from inside his cloak. "Well, since we are a family now, shall we change your surname to Dracula?"

"No," the sisters said in unison.

"We'd like to be called Weird," said Mayrina.

"Ooh, yes! I love it," Mona agreed. "Mona Weird."

"Myrtha Weird," she let it live a moment on her tongue. "It's nice having a surname!"

"It is," Mayrina sighed with content.

"Very well. Cheers to the Weird family!" he said, lifting Van Helsing's ragdoll arm by the sleeve. "Now, allow me to take you to your dessert. I happen to know a place with a Duke who has very aged, well-seasoned blood."

The Weird sisters grinned wickedly. They were finally home.

68

Emily Elledge (28, she/they) is a writer and wannabe illustrator from Mississippi. She lives in her hometown and is a stay-at-home mom.

Not Dead Yet

By Jessica Gleason

Illyana popped her Bubble Yum, its saccharine flavor having worn away hours ago, "I don't know, Camilla. This doesn't seem like a great idea. Don't do this again."

Camilla, wearing her signature scowl, glared at the bright Barbie-esque woman in front of her, "Illyana, it's been well over 100 years. You can't still be this squeamish. Where has your hunger gone?"

"It doesn't have anything to do with being squeamish. I just think we need to keep a low profile, blend in, don't rouse the anger of the natives. You know? I'm tired of picking up and moving every time you have a grand idea and make a buffet out of the locals. It's much harder to do in this modern world, and it's taking a toll on my IG stats." Illyana blew another bubble while admiring her latest manicure, bright pink with extra sparkle. "People have been chasing us with pitchforks and trying to lynch us for decades now. Aren't you tired of that shit?"

Camilla rolled her eyes, not understanding how her sister-wife still maintained so much disgusting humanity. The world was theirs for the taking, and they were entitled to it. Humans were mere ants, suitable for work and excellent as a food source but holding no other real value, "Illyana, you vex me. We are creatures of the night, supernatural beings. We're better, faster, stronger than any of these insignificant people. If I'm hungry, I will eat. You go on and keep posting your vain self-portraits to your tiny computer thing."

"Ugh. You are a dinosaur. Do you know that? They're called "selfies" and I'm making pretty big money by posting them. I'm an influencer. That's important. This is all part of my brand." She huffed, baffled by how out of touch her sister had become. "And I'm not telling you to starve. But, like, you don't have to drain everyone dry. That's just greedy. You know very well that a sip or two will sate your hunger for days. No one has to die. You just enjoy leaving empty carcasses behind like crunched-up human juice boxes. It's not for me. I've learned to control my hunger with no help from you, I might add. You should too. You're being careless."

"I hate that we're bound like this, you know?" Camilla replied, wishing she could break the bond between herself and Illyana, the only two remaining brides of Dracula. But she couldn't. They were linked together for eternity or until one of them expired; Dracula made sure of it.

"What would you do without me here? I'm the only one keeping you from sucking the world dry. When you run out of bodies, you'll be pretty hungry. Did ya ever think of that?" Illyana giggled, attempting to lighten the mood. Camilla was her opposite, brooding and dark and old-fashioned. She'd still be wearing her white bonnet if it wouldn't make her stick out like a sore thumb outside of, say, a historical reenactment or Amish community. Her skirts, and they were always skirts, brushed her ankles stopping just above her sensible black square-toed shoes, and her top was always buttoned right to the nape of her neck. Camilla's thick raven hair was either dangling down her back, a thick-corded braid, or pulled tight and piled on top of her head into a painful-looking bun. She was beautiful, but all fierce, hard lines and no fun.

Illyana, on the other hand, embraced being a modern woman. She cheered when females gained rights in the world, and she jumped at the opportunity to wear skin-tight leather skirts and animal-print tops in the 1980s. New fashion intrigued her, and the short, tight clothing flattered her hourglass figure. The long drapey robes of her past were shed as soon as she was able and despite the fact that she couldn't see herself in the mirror, she had become adept at applying modern makeups, "Maybe we can just go shopping instead?" Illyana suggested, "Your wardrobe sure could use some updating."

Camilla frowned again. "The master would not approve of your embarrassing clothing."

Looking dramatically to her left and then to her right, Illyana replied, "I don't see him here. Do you?"

"It does not matter. We are his brides. We represent him."

Illyana put a supportive hand on her companion's shoulder and looked into her narrow eyes, "Camilla, we are old news. You know very well that Dracula left us long ago. He's a modern man now and has no need for a dwindling bevy of devoted wives."

"Things change. He will call again. He will need our services. There will be bloodletting and sacrifice."

Sighing, Illyana felt that Camilla was a hopeless bore, "No, there won't. He's not out there killing en masse anymore. None of them are. Renfield runs a stupid blog that no one is even reading. Well, maybe I've read it, but no one else is reading it. This is a new age. And I hate to tell you, but 'the Master' has a new girlfriend. We just need to, like, live our own lives. They're a gift. There's so much to see and do and learn if you'd just loosen up a little bit. So, if you're going in *there*," Illyana gestured to the culinary school's test kitchen in front of them, "I'm not coming. I'll have no part in what you're doing. These kids are here to learn. They've done nothing wrong. They're just starting their new independent lives. Do you remember what that was like? Think really hard. There's got to be a shred of humanity in there somewhere. Like, leave them alone."

Camilla stamped her foot and grumbled, "But I'm hungry."

"So, let's go to a frat party tonight, have a few nips, and then move along. Is that so hard?"

"Why would I just sample my meal? I'm entitled to the whole thing."

"No, you're not. We're not entitled to anything. You don't NEED to go around killing folks. You just want to. It's not very lady-like, you know. You're always worried about your pristine conservative image. How would you feel if someone caught you with your fangs out?"

Irate, Camilla screamed in frustration, "Just leave me alone, you idiot. I'll do as I please."

Illyana shrugged and sat at a picnic table in the quad, stretching her legs out and resting them on the bench across the way. "Okay then," Illyana began, heaving a dramatic sigh, "I guess I'll wait here." She unlocked her phone and opened Instagram so she could mindlessly scroll through Reels while Camilla made another careless mess. She'd made so many over the years that Illyana was resigned to the whole ordeal. At least she'd get some solid moon bathing in while her companion wreaked havoc.

When the first scream reverberated out into the night, Illyana rolled her eyes, imagining her idiot sister ripping out another throat, blood spurting across the room, splattering onto the ceiling and splashing down to the floor. She gagged, thoughts of that much blood causing hot bile to rise in her throat. Blood was necessary for their existence, but it didn't mean they needed to decorate with it. Illyana stifled a second gag as the coppery smell wafted from the building, filling her nostrils as it congealed and dried. She much preferred to bewitch a horny lunkhead using her vampiric prowess, sink her teeth in, and have a few gulps to quell her primal hunger, "Ugh. She's so archaic."

When everything began, there were three wives, endlessly hungry and eager to please their master, Count Dracula himself. But times were certainly different. Their countries were war-torn and brutal. A little extra blood wasn't much noticed. Over time, that became less and less true and after their husband had abandoned them to live his new and modern life, they had the choice to change or get left behind. Illyana had chosen to change. Her sister-wives, Silvia and Camilla weren't so eager to step into a new century and away from their precious Vlad.

Placing her head in her hands, silently saying her "sorries" for the crimes of her sister, Illyana hoped it wouldn't come to this, like it had with Silvia. While Silvia and Camilla were both enti-tled and bloodthirsty, thinking themselves above everyone and everything else, that's where the similarities ended. As hard as it was to contemplate, Camilla was the more tolerable of her com-panions.

Silvia was bloodthirsty, but she was also violent and cruel. So, when the bullying became too much for Illyana, when she first considered herself a modern woman worthy of respect, she'd killed Dracula's third wife—staked her in a bout of blind rage—and she'd had no regrets since. Things were better without the cruel tortures Silvia made them endure. Even Camilla had breathed a sigh of relief when they felt the ties that bound them to Silvia sever.

"She's gone," Camilla whispered, "I can't feel her anymore."

Having dusted herself off, no evidence of the crime she'd committed, Illyana embraced her sister, "She is. We're free of her menacing ways."

While they had no physical scars, due to their powers, both sisters could feel the welts from the lashings they'd endured, could smell the sizzle of their own flesh as Silvia branded them over and over again.

"I feel like we should be sad or mourn her loss, because she was a part of us,"

"But you don't want to?" Illyana countered, "And, neither do I. She doesn't deserve it. Be happy she's gone. We can live our lives now, free and unencumbered."

Unfortunately, their camaraderie had been short-lived. Camilla hadn't altered her ways. She was pompous and greedy, violent, and delighted in the suffering of mankind. Illyana saw, firsthand, how humanity was already suffering. She didn't need to contribute to their misery or add to their violence. They killed one another with wild abandon, and they left the weak behind. Sure, there was good too. But Illyana wanted no part in adding to what was already a sad state of affairs.

She'd been violent in her past and had lost the taste for it. Now, she just wanted to enjoy life to the best of her abilities. While her kind wasn't necessarily accepted, it was easy for them to blend in, to exist without disturbing the human ecosystem more than just a little, and there were places where one could live a full and robust life, cities that never slept. Things could be and have been much worse.

Camilla emerged from the building, her garb drenched with the blood of youths, their life force smeared across her angled face. "Now, that was a meal."

"You look disgusting. And now we have to find somewhere else to go. What's wrong with you?"

Camilla sped forward, reaching Illyana in an instant, on a blood-high with heightened abilities. "Sister, you are weak. Look at what this blood has done for me. Why, I could snap you like a twig in mere seconds."

"You could have done that anyway. This is no more than what humans refer to as a sugar rush. You'll crash from your high in minutes and then you'll just want to go massacre more people. It's tedious. Is that all you are? Empty hunger with no soul, no reason for existing?"

Taken aback by her sister's cruelty, Camilla spat a wad of blood-tinged saliva in Illyana's face, "You go too far. How dare you insult me?"

Wiping the offensive spittle from her face, Illyana's rage took over once again, "If the shoe fits, sister. If the shoe fits."

With that, she reached into her Coach bag, pulling out a small worn wooden stake, one she'd whittled herself and had been carrying around for decades. Shock was the first thing to register on Camilla's face. "You wouldn't?"

"I've done it before. I guess I'll have to do it again."

Fear registered next. "No…" Camilla began as the sharp tip of the stake pressed into her pliant flesh, deep into her chest cavity, before finally reaching her vulnerable, cold heart.

"Yes, I took care of our sister. Someone needed to. And now I've got to take care of you too. There's no place in this world for something as soulless and hungry as you are."

Camilla gurgled out a cluster of garbled syllables, not having enough time to form a coherent string of words, before bursting into a cloud of dingy tan-colored powder. The dust fell to the ground, lit by the bright moon, finally settling there across the concrete and manicured grass before being swept away by a rush of wind. "Goodbye sister," Illyana said, mourning the loss just a little this time, before walking down the quad and into the night.

Once she was far enough away from the carnage, she opened her Instagram app, deciding to go live. "Hello, darlings. It's me, your lady of the night, here with a special announcement. I'm on the move again, looking for a new place to call home. Where do the spooky people live? Where are my pastel goths at? I'll be road-tripping to the places you all suggest and hope to see all of your beautiful faces as I adventure across America looking for a new place to call home. Head to my profile and fill out the survey to let me know which places I simply must visit. Love to you all." With a kissing noise and a peace sign, she stopped recording and waited for the results to start pouring in. She thought she might like Portland, but she'd never been.

S itting in bed, next to his new companion, a few hours away along the shores of Lake Michigan, Dracula sat up startled from his reading.

"What is it?" Penelope asked.

"My wife."

She looked at him, incredulous, "Your who and what now?"

"Ahhh…" he said, sheepishly, unable to blush due to the lack of blood flow, "*One* of my wives, rather."

Looking down at the shining purple stone on her own finger, Penelope responded, "Excuse me?"

"Well, you know my story? You've read the book."

Considering Stoker's novel and its contents she nodded solemnly, "I have."

"Then, you know of my brides."

"I mean, I guess, in a cursory way. Are you telling me they're still out there somewhere?"

"Well, one of them is. The other two are no more."

"And you just what? Abandoned them?"

He nodded, ashamed, "Well, more or less. I decided I needed to be a modern man and having a collection of blood-thirsty wives didn't really go with my image. You know?"

"No, I most certainly do not know," she replied, angry and upset by this new information. "We don't abandon the people we love where I'm from."

"Well, I didn't love them. I just wanted them. So, I took them. It was a different time."

Chewing on his declarations, Penelope wondered if she really knew the man she'd married, the one she was very much in love with. "And, what will you do when I no longer suit your needs or fit your image?"

"This. Us. This isn't the same thing."

"How?"

"It just isn't. Okay?"

"Not even a little. So, what about this third wife of yours? Where is she? What is she? Don't you care?"

"Ah, Illyana, no. I think she will be just fine. She's very modern. She's what you might call an influencer."

"And she's not going to come here and wreck our happy home? Or am I the homewrecker in this scenario?"

"Nothing of the sort. I imagine she's off on a new adventure. She'll be just fine."

Penelope crossed her arms, needing time to come to terms with all that had transpired in the last few minutes, before getting up and packing an overnight bag.

"Where are you going? This is preposterous." Dracula said, waving his hands with much fanfare.

"To meet your last remaining wife. Tell me where she's at."

"Oh, boy," Drac replied, thinking this a terrible idea.

Jessica Gleason is a lover of horror and fantasy in their various shapes and forms and can usually be found penning gory tales deep into the night. She enjoys painting monsters with acrylics and singing a mean hair metal karaoke. Her daytime persona teaches college English and Communications in the American Midwest. Her recent releases include "The Dangerous Miss Ventriloquist" and "The Fabulous Miss Fortune" (Evil Cookie Publishing, 2023). For information on her projects, follow her on Instagram (@j.g.writes), where she hosts a monthly horror writer challenge, #WeWriteHorror.

https://jgwrites.carrd.co

Babies in Bags
By Jeremy Megargee

Erma

She can barely meet my eyes, her entire slovenly form slumped down in a snapshot of shame. It's difficult to see her through the smudged plexiglass, and the old corded phone offers only scratchy communication. It has been a struggle to even hear Erma because she speaks meekly, not even an iota of confidence in her words.

She's just a barely visible blob in an orange jumpsuit beyond the glass. Unwashed mousy brown hair, thick bifocals, and teeth that haven't seen a dentist in decades. I'm glad for the barrier between us because I fear her mouth would smell like a sewer up close.

I've been to Lovelock Penitentiary before for my podcast, so I should be accustomed to the poorly funded equipment that haunts this place. It's like a bleak time warp, and no hope is allowed to glimmer here.

I nod to Erma, and with a quick press of a button, we are recording. The guards were begrudgingly willing to mic her up on the other side of the glass, so I'm hopeful that the audio doesn't end up being a total wash.

"Welcome to True Crime Exposed, and I'm your host Mister Moriarty. It's a new month, and we are exploring a grim topic. It is rarely ever even discussed due to the stigma of the word. *Infanticide.* The murder of babies."

I sigh for dramatic effect, and I gesture to Erma with my free hand.

"Thank you for joining us, Erma. I know this isn't an easy thing to talk about. You've been convicted of several counts of infanticide. I suppose one big thing our listeners are curious about, you always hear rumors about how hard it is in prison for someone who kills a small child. That title *baby killer* slips around the neck like a noose, and other inmates seem to hate such a person. Has that been your experience here at Lovelock? Are you demonized above all others because of the nature of your crimes?"

She shuffles on the other side of the glass. Her facial expression doesn't change. I can't help but think she looks like a ruddy toad with bad skin.

"Been hated all my life. No different in here. Mostly I'm invisible. Locked down for 23 hours a day so they don't shank me in the grub hall."

"Lots of isolation. And I'd assume endless time for introspection. Do you ever think about those little ones? Candles snuffed out long before their time."

"Barely remember them. I wasn't me when I did that to them. I was frenzied. I didn't want to smash the heads of those lil' babes. Took no pleasure in cracking them open like eggs."

She stares down at the floor. Her breathing is loud and labored, almost like she's asthmatic.

"I just needed something from them."

"What, Erma? What could you possibly need from a baby fresh out of the womb?"

"You wouldn't understand."

She reaches a meaty hand into her pocket, and when she lifts it back up, she licks something from her thumb. It looks almost like grape jelly, but of a thinner consistency. I needle her for about thirty more minutes, but she has fallen into a sullen silence. Can't squeeze any more juice out of this old piece of rotten fruit.

Doesn't matter. She is only one of three.

Sibyl

"I want your insight, Sibyl. Your sister didn't have much to say. She seemed guilt-ridden and unwilling to talk."

"That woman has the hygiene of an infected big toe and the vocabulary of a kindergartener. Sometimes I think she was adopted. You should have come to me first, handsome."

Sibyl flashes a big beaming smile, and it oozes narcissism. It's immediately apparent how vain she is. Even under prison limitations, she is dolled up. Wavy blonde hair, ocean-blue eyes painted in some rummaged eyeliner, and lips full and moist with gloss.

"Can you tell our listeners why you did what you did? Why target infants? Was it just because they were small and weak, easy targets, or was there a darker design in play?"

She leans back and crosses her arms, eyes tilting up to gaze at the flicking fluorescents. There's a barely concealed perversion swimming in those irises.

"Do you know how trusting a little baby can be? How utterly blameless in this world? They can't speak up to tell someone about atrocities committed against them. They can only babble and ball up lil' soft pink fists. That's why in nature, a predator always goes for the young or the sick or the old, handsome. Quicker. Cleaner. Less chance for something to go wrong."

She licks her lips, and she taps long nails against the plexiglass. They're painted a dark scarlet, and I keep picturing those talons sinking into a newborn's pliable flesh.

"Natural selection. And hell, why do people love veal? There's this element of delicacy. Something fragile and unspoiled just waiting to be taken."

"You speak almost like a cannibal, but there are no records of flesh being consumed after the killings. Did you have fantasies about eating these children?"

Sibyl laughs, and it's comparable to the sound of shattering glass. I feel suddenly lonely in here, nothing but water-stained tiles and a relic of a soda machine somewhere on the far side of the sitting area. She lifts up her index finger and places it across those glossy lips.

"A girl is entitled to a secret or two, isn't she? We're a weird bunch, my sisters and I. I suppose that's why the media ran with the whole "weird sisters" tagline when they finally raided our den."

"That's an interesting choice of words. *Den.* But it wasn't even a house, was it? You and your sisters were squatting in castle ruins. The place is just toppled stone, lost in ivy and moss. I went there once to take photographs, and I barely even found it up in those mountains."

"If only you had seen it in its prime."

"I would imagine if that place had a prime, it was centuries ago. So I don't understand what you mean by that."

She offers up a wink, but nothing more. Sibyl is determined to play coy.

"I'll be speaking to Guinevere next. I've been told she's the wild one of the bunch. Mind putting in a good word for me?"

That jagged laughter again, and I feel like it actually pierces into my skin.

"Unless you want your balls ripped clean from the sack, I'd skip the Guinevere interview. Friendly advice."

Guinevere

Guinevere will not sit. She paces like a leering hyena, and she looks like one too. Deranged lopsided grin, hair a tangled black mop, and little stick figures impaled on pikes tattooed across both of her bare arms. Her eyes are the worst, a jaundiced yellow with tiny black pupils that dagger right through you.

"Do you remember how many, Guinevere? There was never an official count released. But you and your sisters had been raiding cribs for years."

"We never counted. Why bother? Do you count how many steaks you buy each month from the grocery store?"

"I can't see how that's a relevant comparison here."

She rushes at the glass and presses her brow and palms against it. Several whitehead pimples burst on her forehead and ooze down. I've never been so disgusted, and I'm the host of a true crime podcast.

"He'd bring them to us. Usually a few of them wiggling in sacks or discarded plastic bags. You'd never even guess at what they were if you were out and about. Only if a fat little foot with fat little toes thrust up out of the bag. If you saw that, you'd know."

"*He* would bring them? I assume you are referring to this dark figure of mythos that you claim is responsible for what you and your sisters did. There's never been a single scrap of evidence found to suggest that such a person exists. Son of Sam claimed that a demon dog told him to kill. I don't see how this is any different."

Guinevere balls up a fist and begins to lightly pound it on the glass, almost rhythmic. There are more guards lurking in the background than normal because this one is known to be especially violent.

"I miss them, you know? I opened up my cellmate with a razor blade and suckled the night away, but it just wasn't the same. Leathery and used up, no vitality there. But my friend, take it from me, there is nothing like taking an infant inside of yourself. It's a reverse birth. You become the anti-mother. Not there to nurture, but to consume."

Her tongue slips out, far too long for my liking, and she licks at the glass, leaving snail trails of saliva there to drip down as we record.

"You asked how many? You wouldn't believe it. I have devoured entire generations. I have dined on innocence for longer than you have been alive. The next time you see a chubby toddler face on a missing poster, *think of me*. You call it infanticide. I call it a night out drinking with the girls."

She's becoming increasingly agitated, and I'm starting to become concerned that she will attempt to break the glass.

"They're not really dead, you know. That's the sickest part. The part I *love* the most. They're in my veins. All these little unlived lives and unfulfilled memories. I eat babies because I like it. I tear off their soft fat heads and drink them like juice boxes because they taste good."

Guinevere's nostrils flare, and those yellowed eyes grow large with want.

"Your wife has one growing in her belly even now. I can smell the fine hair and unblemished skin. Maybe I'll become mist and pay your house a visit soon."

She is roaring now, spittle flying, and she dive bombs her head into the plexiglass over and over, lacerating her own brow and dragging her own nails impotently against the unyielding glass. She drags her face back and forth, smearing herself and making a blood-stained show for me.

"Maybe at the hour of his birth, I'll have a *taste*."

The guards mercifully drag her away, and I exhale deeply when I stop the recording. I've heard the ramblings of many a nut job while doing this gig, but that one was particularly unsettling.

It's no secret that my wife is pregnant, but it vexes me to know that this madwoman somehow got a hold of that information even while behind bars.

It's dark when I finally leave Lovelock. I make a beeline for my car, eager to get home to my wife and the safety of familiar walls, but something distracts me. I'm not entirely sure why I decide to follow that little twisting wooded trail near the back of the prison. It's a magnetism that lords over me, and curiosity has always been my greatest weakness in this life.

It takes a mile or two before I reach the tree, but for whatever reason, it's hard to judge distances out here. It feels like I've been walking for hours. It is a great lonely dead tree in the center of a clearing, and hundreds of plastic shopping bags hang from the bare branches. The shopping bags are wiggling, and soft mournful cries emerge from them at random intervals.

A dark man stands in front of the tree. He wears a heavy black winter coat with large buttons and a collar that rises about his neck. He looks at me and through me. He is grinning, and the moonlight shows me endless teeth all crowded together in his rictus mouth.

"So kind of you to visit my brides."

"You're not really here. You can't be."

"I am here. I've *always* been here."

He opens his coat to me, and I see only a void.

"And I am thirsty."

Jeremy Megargee has always loved dark fiction. He cut his teeth on R.L Stine's Goosebumps series as a child and a fascination with Stephen King, Jack London, Algernon Blackwood, and many others followed later in life. Jeremy weaves his tales of personal horror from Martinsburg, West Virginia with his cat Lazarus acting as his muse/familiar. He is a native of Appalachia and you can often find him peddling his dark words in various mountain hollers deep within the wilderness.

Cold Shoulders
By Henry Herz

Woodgate, NY

DNR Investigative Services wasn't based in a typical urban high-rise office, but rather at a mansion within a walled rural estate in upstate New York. It was a setting consistent with DNR's billing rates and staffing, which were also far from typical.

Retired U.S. Army Ranger turned DNR executive assistant Ray stopped outside his boss's office. He ran a hand through his blond hair, buttoned his tailored suit jacket, and straightened his azure Hermès silk tie. His employer was a stickler for professional attire and fastidious grooming. Old school.

Ray strode into a large office lined with ebony board and batten paneling. "Good morning, sir. Here's the final report on the Tucker case." He approached his boss's carved mahogany Brobdingnagian desk, dramatically framed by a floor-to-ceiling stained glass window depicting a dragon *rampant guardant*.

His dark-haired employer, wearing a black suite and red tie, had deep gray eyes that suggested an age belied by his trim physique. He looked up from his computer. "Thank you, Ray. You can set it there." He tilted his chin at the front right corner of his meticulous desktop.

The antique Stromberg Carlson model 1179 desk phone rang. The black Bakelite cradle style telephone from 1919 had a round base with nickel-plated finger-wheel.

Ray's eyebrows rose. He'd never heard the phone ring before, and had assumed it was purely decorative. It must be a personal number that few people knew, he concluded.

After considering the phone's insistent ringing, his boss lifted the receiver. "DNR Investigative Services."

Ray's keen ears allowed him to overhear the conversation.

A sultry female voice responded, "Hello. Is this the owner?"

"It is. With whom do I have the pleasure of speaking?"

"My name is Michaela Bercu. I have a rather unusual and sensitive predicament. I have been told on good authority that you excel in resolving such matters."

"You are too kind, Ms. Bercu. What is the nature of your situation?"

"I am afraid it is too delicate to discuss on the phone. Would you be available to come to my office in Utica today?"

"Ah, Ms. Bercu, I regret to say today's schedule is quite full."

Ray winked, recognizing his boss setting the hook.

"Of course," she replied, her voice somehow conveying an alluring smile. "I expected as much from someone with your expertise. But I only need thirty minutes of your time. The matter is quite urgent. I would be willing to compensate for the short notice by paying a full day's rate."

Now it was Ray's boss's eyebrows turn to rise. "Well, I suppose I could alter my schedule given the urgency of your request." He glanced at his platinum and black enamel Patek Philippe 5088/100P Calatrava wristwatch. "Does 2 p.m. suit?"

"Perfectly. My office is suite 230 in the Grifant Office Building. 1428 East-West Arterial Highway. Thank you so much for accommodating my request."

"It is my pleasure, Ms. Bercu." He hung up, easing back in his black and onyx Herman Miller Aeron desk chair.

Ray smiled. "Well played, sir. Even with the forty-minute drive to Utica, you just quadrupled your hourly rate."

"Indeed." His boss nodded. "But it is less about the compensation, and more about divining how seriously the client deems the matter." He leaned forward. "Please update me on the Tucker case."

Half-way through the debriefing, Ray's mobile phone rang. "DNR Investigative Services. How may I help you?" A pause. "Of course, Mr. Torgersen. He's right here." Ray covered his phone's mic. "It's the CEO from Norsemen Cruise Line, sir. It appears they're in need of your advice again." He handed over the phone.

After a brief conversation, his boss hung up. "Well, that is inconvenient timing."

"Sir?"

"It appears our long-standing client needs me to participate in a call with their board of directors at 2 p.m. Today. I cannot decline. Please attend the new client meeting in my stead. Get the details of her situation, but do not commit to the case. I will join you in person if my Norsemen call finishes early."

"Of course, sir. She's likely to be disappointed by your absence."

"Yes. You may convey today's meeting is gratis."

Utica, NY

Ray parked in the Grifant Office Building garage and took the stairs to the second floor. Striding through a worn beige-carpeted hallway, he knocked on the door to suite 230.

"Come in," came that same sultry voice.

Ray entered a tastefully appointed space, its colorful Persian rug, landscape oil paintings, vintage table lamps, and leather-upholstered furniture reminiscent of a cozy living room. He did not notice the tiny surveillance camera hidden within a painting.

An attractive young woman with intense green eyes and a cascade of auburn locks stood from behind a carved wooden desk. Though professionally dressed in a knee-length skirt and forest green button-down blouse that accentuated her eyes, her curves evoked a physical reaction in her visitor.

A woman's voice came through her Bluetooth earpiece. *That is not Him.*

A scowl flitted across her Helen of Troy face. "Hello. Who are you?"

"Ms. Bercu? I'm Ray Renfield from DNR. My employer sends his apologies. He was called away unexpectedly by a long-time client emergency. There will be no charge for today's meeting. How may we help?"

She sat, gesturing with an arm to a guest chair of sienna leather with wooden legs carved to resemble vines. "Just a moment, please." She flipped through a folder to buy herself time to listen to her earpiece.

Just give him the alibi and let him go, Verona, advised the female voice. *We shall leave the adjacent suite and head back to the warehouse. See if you can learn anything useful.*

Verona set down the folder. "Thank you for your patience, Ray."

Hearing her speak his name felt like she brushed his ear with her full lips.

She detailed her fabricated predicament, stopping occasionally to answer Ray's questions. She admired the man's muscular six-foot-tall frame.

Verona rose, gliding to a second guest chair closer to Ray, her movements fluid and graceful as a hunting cat's.

Ray's eyes dilated, as did another part of his anatomy. He tried to distract himself from her allure by telling a joke.

She giggled, placing a hand on Ray's knee. "I find a sense of humor attractive."

Tensing, Ray replied. "No offense, Ms. Bercu. You are a beautiful woman, but I have a girlfriend."

She gave a smile that warmed him down to his toes. "I do not mind sharing."

Ray's pulse raced at the sudden realization he was in far greater danger than just infidelity. He tried to stand, but his legs wouldn't respond. "I'm sorry, but—" He lost the power of speech when she leaned in and breathed softly on his neck.

"Relax, Ray."

His eyes rolled up and his limbs went limp.

At a knock at the door, her lips pulled back to reveal fangs, her hunger barely under control.

The locked doorknob rattled as the visitor tried to open the door.

"I am with a client," she managed. "Please call for an appointment."

The door burst open, the jamb splintered. Ray's boss sniffed the air like a wolf. His eyes narrowed.

Verona snarled, bearing her fangs. "YOU!" She backhanded Ray to the floor and leaped behind her desk. "He's here!" she said, yanking open a drawer.

Dracula rushed to his assistant lying senseless on the rug, his back to the desk.

Snatching a sharp wooden stake from the drawer, Verona raised it and charged.

In the blink of an eye, Dracula gripped the fallen chair, spun, and thrust with superhuman strength. One of the chair legs punched through Verona's chest, pinning her like a butterfly specimen.

She gasped and fell writhing to the floor when Dracula released the chair. No blood flowed from her grievous wound.

Dracula's eyes widened in recognition. He knelt, seizing Verona's shoulders in an iron grip. "Why are you here? What do you want with me?"

Struggling to form the words, Verona whispered. "You selfish monster. Even now, you do not apologize for abandoning us." Her eyes dimmed. Her body slackened and turned to dark, acrid smoke.

"Boss? Who … What?"

Dracula knelt by his prostrate assistant. "Just lie there until your head clears, Ray." Inspecting his assistant's neck, Dracula's brow wrinkles faded when he noted no puncture wounds. "That was Verona. She, Aleera, and Marishka were vampire brides I left behind long ago in Transylvania to pursue fresh prey in London. As you know, I now feed only upon the willing. But it would seem my dark past has caught up with me yet again. I regret my malevolent choices, but even a vampire lord cannot turn back the hands of time."

Ray nodded. "How … how did you get here so quickly, sir?"

"Something about Ms. Bercu's voice seemed familiar. So, I drove here in advance and joined the Norsemen teleconference from my car." He helped Ray to his unsteady feet. "It may take several hours for your dizziness to fully pass. I shall take you home and arrange for a driver to collect your Jaguar."

"Thank you, sir."

Dracula aided his staggering assistant to the garage and into the passenger seat of a burgundy McLaren F1. Not completely old school.

Woodgate, NY—The Next Day

Ray entered Dracula's office. "Good news, sir. I was able to track down the name and address of the business entity that rented the Utica office where I was attacked. A firm named Wallachian Imports owns a warehouse in Rome, NY."

"Well done, Ray. Unfortunately, I suspect that when Verona said, 'He's here,' she was alerting the other two brides. It is clear to me they will continue to seek vengeance against me. That also puts you in grave danger. A preemptive strike by us seems, sadly, the only prudent option. Assemble the necessary equipment for a noon raid tomorrow. It's a Saturday, and that should lessen the likelihood of innocent human workers at the warehouse. Further, by assaulting them in daytime, we deprive them of the ability to shift form. If fortune favors us, we will find their coffins. If not, we may still find clues as to their resting place. Find out if the building exterior is concrete, brick, stucco, metal, or something else."

After researching the warehouse construction, Ray rented a van and spent two hours loading it with equipment they'd need, and some they might not. While they had the element of surprise, one can never be too careful when facing vampires.

Rome, NY—The Next Day

Gray, overcast skies threatened rain the entire fifty-minute drive, but the only precipitation was a brief drizzle as Dracula and Ray neared Rome.

"This van handles and accelerates like a freighter, boss."

"Yes, but it does offer cargo capacity for all your toys, Ray."

Wallachian Imports was located on Milton Avenue, not far from Griffiss International Airport.

Ray parked two blocks from the warehouse. He unpacked and launched a short-range reconnaissance drone. After it circled the single-story target twice, he flew it back, stowing it in the rear of the van.

"Good news, sir. The drone video feed didn't show anyone entering or leaving the building. Hopefully, there aren't any civilians inside. All the windows have iron security bars on the outside and are shuttered on the inside. There's a main entrance on the street and another on the alley at the back."

Dracula patted Ray's back. "Very good. Let us gear up, as they say."

The pair strapped on their equipment in the back of the van. Fifteen minutes later, Dracula emerged, wearing a black leather duster and stylish fedora. He hooked a black umbrella over an arm. "Hazard pay applies today, Ray."

Ray nodded, his face grim. A long gray raincoat and wide-brimmed gambler hat concealed his kit. "Sir, I can probably pick the lock on the rear entrance, but in all likelihood, the door has a security alarm. And if it was my lair, I'd also have surveillance cameras monitoring both entrances. If they're really thorough, the back door will be boobytrapped."

"I intend to circumvent the door altogether." Dracula shrugged. "But there is nothing we can do about a hidden camera, except to breach expeditiously. Fortunately, as you learned, the walls are stucco, not masonry. Follow me."

Dracula led them down the alley to the rear entrance. Ten feet to the right of the door, he set down his umbrella and drew a cinquedea from a sheath at his waist, the broad dagger's blade nearly triangular in shape. Waiting for a jet takeoff to mask the noise, he stabbed the cinquedea with inhuman strength through the building's stucco exterior at a height of three feet. He repeated the process three times, dislodging a six-inch square piece. Sheathing his blade, he inserted a hand into the gap and ripped a larger chunk of the wall outward. Within a minute, he had torn open a three-foot high by two-foot wide opening. "Follow me." He picked up his umbrella and entered.

Ray followed him through the wall into what turned out to be an unoccupied office. He advanced to the office's interior door and placed an ear against the wood. He shook his head to convey hearing nothing. Cracking the door open an inch, he peered through the gap. The space beyond was utterly dark, so he shut the door. "I can't see anything," he whispered. "One sec, boss." Ray removed his hat, revealing an AN/PVS-31 binocular night vision device. Settling it in place over his eyes, he activated it, eased open the door, and crept through.

Dracula needed no such assistance to see in the dark. He followed Ray into a large, high-ceilinged space that seemed to account for a majority of the warehouse's square footage.

Ray smelled plywood and petrichor. His BNVD revealed stacked rows of hundreds of crates, each large enough to accommodate a sleeping vampire, forming a miniature wooden city. "Shit," he whispered. "Any of those could be coffins. Where do we even start?"

"Your question is moot, Ray. We have lost the element of surprise." Dracula pointed to two male figures who appeared at the far side of the space, advancing toward them. He sniffed. "They are not human. It would appear the brides recruited a pair of drudges."

Ray scowled, even though he hadn't held out much hope of raiding a vampire lair without being detected. Despite his training and extensive experience fighting undead, he shivered. Only a fool faced vampires without dread and a reminder of their own mortality.

"Not drudges, old man. Allies," replied a black-haired vampire who looked no older than twenty. Both vampires halted thirty feet away. "The brides have wanted to get even with you for a long time. They didn't count on you destroying Verona—they were some kind of pissed—but you still fell into their trap by coming here. What's that saying about vengeance, Todd?" he asked his red-headed comrade.

"Shit if I know, dude."

Dracula answered, "La vengeance est un plat qui se mange froide." When the black-haired vampire just stared, he added, "Vengeance is a dish best served cold. It is from Pierre Choderlos de Laclos's 1782 epistolary novel *Les Liaisons Dangereuses*."

"Well, look at that. The limp old bloodsucker's also a walking encyclopedia. I bet you're real fun at parties."

Ray bristled at the insult to his master. He sidestepped ten feet away from Dracula and whipped off his raincoat. A holster on his left hip held a 9mm Glock 17 pistol with a thirteen-round magazine. A Smith & Wesson Model 500 five-shot revolver with a ported 7.5" barrel hung at his right hip. Both safeties were already off, a necessary risk. A camouflaged nylon tactical vest with Modular Lightweight Load-carrying Equipment webbing covered his torso. Spare magazines for the Glock, speed loaders for the revolver, pepper spray, a crowbar, and a sheathed M3 trench knife hung from the vest. Most importantly, the vest's webbing prominently displayed three silver crucifixes on Ray's chest and three on his back.

One can never be too careful when facing vampires.

The redhead, Todd, hissed at Ray's crosses, then sneered. "Bullets? Pepper spray?" He glanced at his companion. "Don, this dude doesn't know anything about vampires."

Ray removed the pepper spray from his vest with his left hand. His right hand drifted to the revolver grip.

Dracula doffed his duster with a flourish, revealing a high-collared loose-fitting shirt. He pulled a hidden sword from his umbrella. Old school. He drew the cinquedea from its sheath with his left hand. "Have you two drudges finished your banal blathering?"

Don snarled. "I'll end the pompous pirate. Todd, you drain the human." He withdrew two foot-long wooden stakes from the rear of his belt.

"On it, bro."

As Don charged Dracula, Todd rushed at Ray. Of course, overcoming a resolute human wearing repelling crosses and trained to avoid direct eye contact is easier said than done. Judging by his facial expression, this realization struck Todd about the same time as a burning stream of garlic solution from Ray's pepper spray dispenser.

Ray nimbly sidestepped the temporarily blinded oncoming vampire like a toreador.

Todd screamed in agony, stumbling to a halt ten feet beyond Ray. "I'm gonna tear you into pieces, you pathetic human! And I'll do it slowly, so you can watch." He pulled up his shirt to wipe the garlic spray from his eyes.

Taking careful aim, Ray fired the revolver, his eyes shutting at the brilliant flash in the darkness. The boom from the powerful handgun echoed through the warehouse. The round struck just right of the sternum, knocking Todd back a pace.

"Bullets? Seriously, dude? You know we don't have circulatory or respiratory systems, right?"

Ray fired again, this time with better aim, just to the left of the sternum.

The redhead wasn't wrong about traditional bullets' inability to kill vampires. That's why the Smith & Wesson was loaded with custom-made magnum rounds of half-inch-diameter sharpened Brazilian olive wood. A thin layer of steel sheathed each projectile to prevent splintering when fired and striking the target. Two-thousand-feet per second stakes.

One can never be too careful when facing vampires.

Todd's eyes widened. He toppled backward to the floor, vanishing into foul-smelling smoke.

Ray shifted his focus to his master. Don was faster than Dracula, but skillful sword slashes forced the younger vampire to keep his distance. As Ray considered how to help, something struck between his shoulder blades with terrible velocity. The impact cracked ribs, knocked the wind out of him, and threw him onto his face. A now-blunted wooden stake clattered to the warehouse floor. He raised his head, shaking it to clear the pain.

"Well, well. That is surprising," said Aleera, a voluptuous redhead even more attractive than Verona, if that were possible. "When I hurl a stake at someone, it usually emerges on the opposite side of their body. Just a minor annoyance, though." She closed her eerie pale blue eyes momentarily and mumbled. "There. I have summoned some wolves to entertain you."

With Dracula's attention focused on a flurry of stabbing attacks by the dark-haired vampire, he failed to notice raven-haired Marishka creep up and jam a stake into his back.

The ceramic-coated compressed-polyethylene cuirass and gorget armor concealed under Dracula's flowing shirt turned the blow. Not completely old school.

Ducking a chest-high thrust from Don, Dracula pivoted and launched a backhand slash that severed Marishka's right hand, still holding the blunted stake.

She howled in anguish, though no blood pumped from her undead wrist. Despite the pain, the wound was primarily an annoyance, as vampires healed from mundane weapon wounds in minutes.

At her sister's cry of distress, Aleera faced Dracula and drew a stake from her belt. She screamed with fury and stormed at her maker.

Still stunned, Ray rolled onto his back and sat up, struggling to fill his lungs. Before he could recover sufficiently to aid his master, canine growling snared his attention. Three large black and gray wolves raced toward him.

Ray drew his Glock. From his position on the floor, he managed to get off three rounds, killing one wolf before the other two were on him. At the last second, he pivoted to protect his head and right side of his body.

One wolf clamped its teeth on his left shin, the other, his left forearm. The slavering beasts jerked their jaws to and fro. The violent wrenching would have torn apart the flesh of unarmored prey. But the intense pressure from the wolves' fangs couldn't penetrate the Kevlar chainmail shark suit Ray wore under his clothing. The same chainmail that had prevented the vampire's stake from skewering him. Ray fired two 9mm rounds into each wolf's head. The silver-tipped bullets were overkill for normal wolves.

Facing three undead opponents, Dracula backed into a corner formed by stacked wooden crates. The greater reach of his sword kept his foes at bay for the moment.

"If his back is armored, so is his chest!" cried Marishka, gritting against the pain. She snatched up the dropped stake with her left hand. "Stab out his eyes and then we can tear off his head!"

Ray struggled to his feet roughly twenty feet from the melee. He assessed using garlic spray with the vampires so close to Dracula as too risky. The odds of him shooting a fast-dodging vampire in the heart were nearly zero, so he changed tactics. He rapid-fired the Glock at Don's legs. Four shots missed, but the fifth shattered the vampire's left kneecap, causing him to cry out and tumble to the floor.

At the sound of gunfire, Marishka rotated toward Ray, her honey-brown eyes no longer seductive, instead glaring with murderous intent.

Ray averted his gaze and holstered his Glock. Readying for her charge, he snatched the garlic spray with his left hand and drew the revolver with his right.

Dracula took advantage of his opponent's momentary distraction. He jabbed at Aleera, who retreated a step. He spun and slashed, parting Marishka's head from her shoulders.

Marishka's body crumpled to the floor. Dark smoke marked her passage into Hell.

"No!" screamed Aleera.

Dracula advanced, and she retreated out of the reach of his longer weapon.

Don scrambled to his unwounded knee, hissing as Ray approached. "Fight fair. Give me a minute."

"Fight fair? I know plenty about vampires. Say hello to my little friend." Ray sprayed garlic into Don's face. As the incapacitated vampire slipped to the floor, writhing in agony, Ray emptied his revolver into Don's chest. The third round pierced his heart.

"Always wanted to say that." Ray reloaded as Don disintegrated into smoke. He crossed to where Dracula had the hissing Aleera backed into a corner like a trapped badger. "All clear behind you, boss."

"Well done, Ray," replied Dracula, never taking his eyes from the cornered vampire.

"You self-centered bastard!" cried Aleera. "You made us dependent on you and then left us without so much as a farewell to fend for ourselves. Your Romani refused to serve us, and we were forced to live underground like rats, feeding on carrion." She spat.

Dracula bowed his head. "I am guilty of abandoning my brides for London, and for that I rue my selfish decision. You may not believe it, but I have changed since then. I have foresworn my old ways, only drinking blood from a willing Renfield, never enough to turn him. I deeply regret having to destroy Verona and Marishka, but I had no choice."

Aleera glared. "Just like you offered us no alternative? Your unbeating heart is as cold as stone."

Dracula tilted his head. "I am offering you a choice now. You could adopt my way of life and have sanctuary at my mansion."

"Sipping rationed blood like a pathetic wretch? Vampires are predators, not scavengers. What is the other choice?"

Dracula shrugged, the alternative obvious.

Fury consumed Aleena, hatred marring her ravishing face. She snarled and flung herself at Dracula, choosing the alternative. Unflinching, Dracula swept off her head with his sword.

"Ah, Ray," he sighed at the smoke. "What a piteous turn of events. The depraved loans I took long ago have demanded repayment with usurious interest."

Ray winced and staggered. "I may need some help getting back to the van, boss. Aleera smacked me pretty hard, and I'm having trouble breathing. Is it okay if I call in sick tomorrow?"

Dracula nodded, easing Ray into a sitting position. "You may have as much time as you need. Right now, I shall take you to a hospital." Wait here while I bring the van to the rear entrance.

He soon returned.

"Some prescription-strength painkillers would be great right about now, boss," Ray said as Dracula loaded him into the van. "Luckily, Rome Memorial Hospital's only five minutes away, boss. Head east and turn right on Broadway."

Dracula started the vehicle and made the turn. "You were correct, Ray. This van does not quite corner like my McLaren."

Author Notes

This is the fourth adventure of occult detectives Dracula and Ray Renfield, whose covert exploits are documented in *Norsemen Cruise Line*, Dracula Beyond Stoker issue #1, *Don't Mess With a Renfield*, Dracula Beyond Stoker issue #2, and *Loose End*, Dracula Beyond Stoker issue #3.

The story title is a wink at the brides' undead nature, as well as how Dracula abandoned them when he traveled to London. DNR is a playful reference to Dracula & Renfield, as well as the medical term, "do not resuscitate." The Michaela Bercu character honors the name of an actress who portrayed one of the brides in the 1992 movie, *Bram Stoker's Dracula*. East-West Arterial Highway is an actual road in Utica, NY. I couldn't resist "arterial" as a street for a Dracula story, and 1428 is Vlad the Impaler's estimated birth year. The bride character names Verona, Aleera, and Marishka match those used in the 2004 film *Van Helsing*. Wallachian Imports is a wink at Vlad the Impaler's historical rule as *Voivode* (warlord) of Wallachia. "Say hello to my little friend" is a quote from the 1983 movie, *Scarface*.

Henry Herz's stories will/have appeared in Daily Science Fiction, Weird Tales, Metastellar, Highlights for Children, Ladybug Magazine, and anthologies from Albert Whitman & Co., Blackstone Publishing, Brigid's Gate Press, Air and Nothingness Press, Baen Books, Titan Books, and elsewhere. He's edited six anthologies and written twelve picture books, including the critically acclaimed I Am Smoke. www.henryherz.com

The Far City
By José Panbehchi

Coney Island, 1980

Valeria Navarra looked over her costume store crystal ball and knew that the mark sitting across from her was too smart and too rich to play hero.

Not rich enough for the Master to want to keep him as a bill paying pet, his sweat stained blazer made that obvious. But from the way he asked about triumph like he was some Roman conqueror and kept his eyes off of Sdenka's low cut dress when she offered him tea, Val knew he made too much to think with his Johnson and actually buy into "the hero game." Meaning when the crying blonde came in from the rain through the Fortune Teller's door, he didn't spare her a glance.

"Help me." She pushed wet hair out of her eyes and leaned against the wine-colored wall. She wore a faded yellow blouse that had specks of dried blood, and torn jeans.

In the time Val had known her, Countess Dolingen needed theatrics to satisfy her peculiar tastes. But Val knew that no matter how much rainwater mixed with tears that Dolly got on the carpet, she'd lose interest in this one the second he opened his mouth.

Sdenka Blagojevich came into the parlor through the curtain behind Val with a Turkish kettle full of Lipton. She acted surprised enough to see Dolly and went to her with a towel to dry her face.

"Madam, are you well?" Sdenka asked.

"You gotta help me, he's lost control—"

"Madame Navarra, please continue." The man took out a cigarette case from his pocket, took two out, and gave one to Val. They weren't high end, but they were good enough.

"Apologies, Mr. Lennox, perhaps we should assist this young woman first." Said Val, trying to play up her old accent. "The spirit realm prefers a small audience."

"You got a telephone?" He asked. Val shook her head and he sighed.

"Please, mister. I can't go home, my husband's out there and he said he'd kill me."

Lennox turned on the stool he was sitting on to face Dolly, reached into his pocket, and put something into her hand.

"Here's a dime. There're payphones on the boardwalk."

Val had to bite her tongue to keep from laughing; it served Dolly right not listening for the tarot cards she drew. There was a microphone in the crystal ball for a reason. If she had, she'd have gone to the Master and let Val and Sdenka bleed this one.

"But he's after me." Dolly said, unable to hide the confusion from her voice.

"Call the police." Lennox took a drag on his cigarette and turned to face Val again. "Now, Madame Navarra, show me some fortune."

Val pulled the nine of cups from the deck of Tarot cards. Wealth, fortune, more of what he wanted to hear.

"Yes Mr. Lennox, in your present, I do see fortune. You savor the spoils of those you best. Pardon me, you haven't gotten your tea." Val clapped her hands and Sdenka came back to the table to pour.

"I don't—" Sdenka poured before he could finish, and he sighed. "You said that was my present, I know that because I work hard for what I have. What I want to know is how this next case is going to leave me. Tell me what's next."

"Very well." Val placed a ten of swords on the table, and Lennox flinched at the sight of a man lying on the ground with ten swords sticking out of his back.

"The hell's that supposed to mean?"

"It means that with every high comes a low, Mr. Lennox." Val clicked her heel against one of the table legs. Sdenka's arm shot out and she hit the side of Lennox's head.

He fell off his stool and dropped to his knees, stars in his eyes.

"I'm going to have you all arrested." Most men would've been knocked out, but he was still up.

"Then call the police." Said Sdenka. She slashed the side of his neck with fingernails the size of pocket knives. A soft spray of blood hit Sdenka in the face, but she didn't dare move.

Lennox brought his hand to his throat, his eyes watering. He gasped for air and dropped to all fours, bleeding.

Val felt her fangs split gum tissue in her mouth as they engorged with anticipation. It'd been too long since the Master and Dolly permitted her to feed. But under the Master's word, she could not move first. That was for the First Bride.

"Yours is the right to begin." Said Val, dropping the fortune teller act. "We should act quick—" Before Val could finish, Dolly raised a hand to silence her.

Dolly passed Val and Sdenka, gripped the crown of Lennox's balding head, and twisted.

He fell to the floor, his chest down and his face up. Blood colored spittle foamed at the side of his mouth.

"Fuck you, Dolly."

Val pounced on him like a starving alley cat. She tried sucking as much blood as she could before death fully took him. She told herself that the taste reminded her of home, of what it was like to feel the sun on her skin. But it didn't. Any joy from that man's blood was an echo of a memory. Then she tasted him die.

She spat out what was in her mouth, trying not to retch up what little had gone into her stomach. He was nothing but bile now.

"I told you to bring me a fighter I could share with the Count." Dolly sauntered to the stool Lennox had been on and threw a towel at Sdenka. "Clean yourself up."

"You didn't listen." Said Val, pointing to the crystal ball and panting. "I never pulled 'The Fool,' you shouldn't have even come."

"It's not my job to understand witchcraft, Valeria. You're the one whose been tied to a stake, not me."

"And that was your code, not mine." Val never used cards or a ball as a Sorginak during Akelarre, she'd modeled her entire act on a psychic she'd known who performed in Dreamland. "Now what're we supposed to do?"

"I have not fed for a week." Said Sdenka. She'd wiped her face with the tea towel and cried as she stared at the drying blood.

"Then find someone who'd promise to fight the Count for me. Tomorrow."

"What?" Asked Sdenka, wiping blood tears from her eyes. "It is not enough time."

"Then starve."

"Where are we supposed to find this sap?" Asked Val. Gone were the days of nameless sailors who could disappear.

"That's your business, not mine."

"Bullshit it's not. You've gotta eat sometime too, Dolly. We need each other." Val went to Sdenka and held her trembling hands.

"You need me. I can hunt alone."

"I've seen you hunt, Countess, and the Master commanded no more children until the heat's off." One dead kid can be explained away by a bad amusement park ride. Three dead kids brought too many cops for Detective Hopkinsto distract. There'd been too many cops for months.

"I know the Count's commands." Dolly glared at Val and Sdenka. "I speak his word, not you. Or have you forgotten your place, witch?" There she was. Almost a century in America, and still, the second Dolly got mad she spoke like a mad Styrian aristocrat. That certainly helped the Master when he picked her as First Bride. "Well?" Dolly's eyes turned red, and her fingernails grew.

"No, my Lady." Val curtsied and gritted her teeth.

"Tomorrow." Dolly said, then left.

Sdenka soaked the bloodied towel in the Motel room shower and was wringing it into her mouth, hoping to taste Lennox's blood. Val sat on the bed next to Lennox's body, smoking his cigarettes and going through his wallet. They'd moved him into the Flying Carpet Inn and away from their store front in the Jupiter Park section of the Boardwalk. Matthew Hopkins, a Brooklyn West homicide detective in the thrall of the Master, had suggested the place. He was on tour today, so he'd be the one taking it when the call came in and he'd make things go smooth.

"Sorry for jumping on him, Enk." Said Val, which was half true. It'd been two weeks since Val fed as opposed to Sdenka's one, despite Val being Second Bride. "If it's any consolation, he tasted like shit."

"Now he tastes like cotton." Sdenka said from the bathroom. Val heard her spit, and she chuckled.

"An improvement." It looked like Lennox was a lawyer according to his AmEx. He must've paid extra for the "Esq." at the end of his name. Aside from the credit card, there was a driver's license, $187, and a condom in the wallet. That made staging easier. She tore open the wrapper but didn't take it out, dropped it next to his knees, and pulled down his pants. She went to the evidence bag Hopkins had given her, pulled out an empty morphine vial, and placed it on the bedside table along with a broken syringe.

Hopkins would see to it that the cops would peg Lennox as a John who got beaten then slashed by a junkie's pimp for non-payment. They'd rubber stamp it, they'd go off hunting again, and this was simply becoming too much work for too little reward.

"I'm tired of this, Enk." Val said, stubbing out the cigarette.

"Do you want me to finish?"

"No, not that it's—" The phone rang. Val let it ring seven times before picking up. "Neptune's Pizza, how can I help you?"

"Checking up on an order." It was Hopkins, likely calling from a pay phone away from his precinct or apartment. "My wife called more than 30 minutes ago; is it free now?" Were they finished yet? He needed to know when to call it in.

"No, we got the call at 8:30, we're still making it. She ordered a pie with extra cheese, anchovies on the side, no garlic." One dead male, still finishing up, staged like a robbery, no witnesses.

"Right. Got any soda?" Injuries?

"We've got diet, and cherry cola." Broken neck and a slashed throat.

"Those are fine, but do you have any ginger ale? Wife's got a stomach ache." Nothing suspicious with the injuries. Did feed?

"We're out." No.

"Shit. Did she give you a card or am I paying the driver in cash?" Was it a nobody or a somebody?

"I've got an AmEx for 'Duncan Lennox, Esq.' is that you?" This is just some ambulance chaser, right?

Hopkins said nothing.

"Sir? Would you rather pay in cash?" Is this someone?

"I'm about to drive home so I'll just pick it up. You're on Surf Avenue, right?" Get out now, meet up on Surf Ave.

"Yes, how long—?"

"Now."

Val and Sdenka were in a diner catty-corner from Nathan's. The radio on the counter was playing the Mets game, and they were losing. Val nursed a coffee that she pretended to drink and kept looking for Hopkins to show.

In the distance, she saw the Ferris Wheel lit in bright colors standing above a sea of carnival games, food stands, and broken-down barflies stumbling about on a Friday night. Hunting should have been easy. Catch a drunk, bleed him some, leave him against a door, and he'd blame it on a hangover come morning. No bodies, no new competitors, easy. But Dolly wanted to kill strapping young fools.

"We're fucked." Said Val.

"We don't know that. We don't know anything."

"We know enough. This is all her fault whatever it is. She's fucking useless anyway, Enk. She doesn't do what we do and at this point, I'm pretty sure she can't." They'd had this conversation every three months for 86 years.

"She can, she has done this longer than us." Sdenka motioned to the jumpy looking fry cook smoking outside, and Val shook her head. She'd seen him before and he'd been shooting up after his shifts and was stealing from the till to keep it up. Dolly didn't eat smackheads.

"We've done all the work since London. All she does is sit in her box and whine because we don't know which of her rules she's arbitrarily changed. And all she has to do is pout and her husband will cave." Val stopped herself from saying, "the Master will feed her someone," in case anyone was listening. "Now look where it's gotten us." The thought of Lennox being someone connected made her worried about running again.

"What can we do? She is First Bride." Val shushed her, but Sdenka'd already said Dolly's title. Val scanned the diner and saw nobody was looking. She hoped that if anyone had heard Sdenka, they thought it was either some religious or sex thing.

"She's awful. I wish you'd met Clarimonde."

"You have never said what happened to her." Said Sdenka. What happened to the last First Bride made Val sad. Clarimonde saved Val from the Inquisitor's stake; and even if survival in undeath forced her to renounce Mari and Suugar, she'd been Val's friend.

"Forget it." It annoyed her enough to have to relive this every time they found some idiot for Dolly to kill.

"Val, you talk about her enough. She meant a great deal to you, and she's gone. You can tell me." At this point, she was tired of dodging the question.

"She fell in love with a priest." The thought of Father Romuald Grandier made her mad, so she looked out the window for a moment scowling.

"What?"

"She wanted out, and asshole wanted to save her from what was going on at home." A man of God who'd throw it all away to try and save a vampire woman from the Master was an idiot. "They tried running, but when Dolly found out, she told her husband and he—" Val picked up a butter knife and mocked stabbing herself in the heart.

"Goodness." Said Sdenka sinking into her side of the booth.

"And that's where we get the hero game, she loves to relive it."

The front door opened and in walked Matthew Hopkins. He wore a tan raincoat over a cheap suit, the only embellishment he had that showed he was in the Master's employ was a blue silk tie.

"It's been an hour and a half, Matt."

"Then the pizza's free." He took off his raincoat, hung it on a hook on one of the booths, and sat. "Where's Dolly?"

"Splitting the atom, who knows."

"And the boss?" He took the cold coffee from in front of Val and downed it in two swallows. He normally didn't act this way because of a corpse. Normally he was a professional, that's what she liked about him.

"What's wrong, Matthew?" Asked Sdenka.

"Where's the boss?"

"In the city; apartment hunting. I'm next in command, what's wrong?"

"The guy was somebody."

"Cop?"

"Worse. This won't die." Hopkins looked over to a waitress who was behind the counter. "Hey, miss, my entire team sucks, go Mets. Can you switch to the news?"

"Whatever." She turned the knob and on came the news channel.

"Once again, we're being told that assistant district attorney Duncan Lennox has been found murdered in Coney Island, in what appears to be a robbery gone wrong. Police have little information at this time."

Val felt cold.

"We have been with Police before." Said Sdenka.

"Yeah, and after some saber rattling, I'd scoop some turnstile jumper off the street and punch his teeth out till he confessed."

"Why's ADA Lennox different, Matt?"

"He was a murder DA, and he was looking into the Scream-O-Rama kids."

"Shush." Val barred her fangs at Hopkins quickly and put them away. "How would that tie to us?"

"They found new evidence."

"We can't be photographed."

"No, but you still have finger prints. And hair. Thank you both for wearing gloves, but they found two sets of prints and blonde hairs."

"Where were you?"

"Trying my best to throw them off the scent. But none of the skells I could feed Lennox had long blonde hair. The boys in blue are going to be looking for a blonde."

"What do we do now?" Asked Sdenka.

"Leave, stay low for a while." Hopkins motioned for the bill and left some cash on the table.

"Scared, Detective Hopkins?" Asked Val.

"I'm not on this one, there were already too many eyes on Jupiter Park, and this makes it worse. Fucking Ed Koch put my Captain on this personally, and he's seen enough of these to know the junkie shit's fake."

"Well running's not an option, Dolly didn't even take to this one. We need to find someone else."

"Shit." Hopkins brought a hand to his forehead. "The last thing you three need is another body in Coney Island."

"We just need a plan." Said Val.

"Well think one up soon, because if they get a daytime warrant for the Scream-O-Rama, they're going to find your coffins."

Just then, three stone-faced cops walked into the diner, followed by the fry cook. Val, Sdenka, and Hopkins froze.

The cops walked past their booth and went up to the counter, sharing some quiet words with the waitress. She motioned her head to the back, and the three uniforms walked into the kitchen.

Five minutes felt like five hours, but when they came out, a girl in cooks whites was in handcuffs screaming about how the cook and the other girl had set her up and that she hadn't taken the money. She struggled, and a small bag of white powder fell to the ground.

As they took the girl, Val could see the waitress behind the counter stroke her apron pocket and then go back into the kitchen with the fry cook.

"Maybe we let them find the coffins." Said Val.

"What?" Asked Sdenka.

"Hear me out."

Val couldn't sleep. It was the waiting that got to her in that dirt filled box. The times when she couldn't sleep and just let herself feel the imported dirt was one of the few times that she actually was able to feel like she was still home in the Basque Country.

It'd taken almost till dawn to convince Hopkins to go along with the plan. They'd been cleaning up the Fortune Telling parlor, making sure to preserve only the pieces of evidence that they needed.

"I swore my life to him, to all of you." He said. "And that includes her especially. She is First Bride."

"That's a made-up title and I'm tired of it. You swore that because you wanted to live forever, Matt and that's not going to happen with Count Dracula." She hadn't spoken the Master's name in almost two hundred years, but it felt good to throw off the yoke of control, at least for a moment. "Do you know how many of you there've been? How many do you think he's actually turned?"

Part of them always know. It's a small part, but it's there. And he tried to fight it but couldn't.

"So that's it? Turn them in? Rikers isn't going to hold them, and they'll kill us."

"Not if they're only bodies."

"Fucking Christ, Val."

"She's just going to keep leaving bodies and if she's gone and he isn't, he'll just find another girl who'll do the same."

"And if I kill them?"

"Then we're free. I'll give you what you want because you're not stupid."

"This is stupid."

"Then what do you suggest?"

"Run. Just run."

Val thought of Clarimonde and thought that Father Romuald must have told her something similar.

"I can't. Matt, Dracula and Dolly's shadow has blocked the sun from me for so long, that even if I wanted to run, with them still walking I don't think I could find the way."

"We can't get out of this otherwise. The NYPD's wants someone for this, this is a DA who was looking for a kid killer."

"They'll get someone."

"With stakes through their hearts?"

"No. There's more than one way to kill someone like me."

"Like how?"

"Fire. Dreamland burned down and it threw the cops off our scent then. But if they find evidence in the rubble, they'll have their answer."

"You think that will work?"

"They were the only ones who handled those kids without gloves, and she grabbed Lennox's head. Like you said, we still have prints. Hair. If Scream-O-Rama burns, they'll look through the rubble and they'll match it up."

Hopkins put out a cigarette on the Fortune Teller's table and looked her in the eye.

"And I can trust you to make me like you, Val?"

"You're like me enough, Matt. You just need one more step."

The kiss was mechanical for her. She liked Matt well enough, but she needed to keep her wits about her.

Before dawn, Sdenka told Dolly and the Master that she would bring someone when dusk fell. It was a going away gift as the Master had found a new lair in Manhattan and would be moving his coffin.

The man who would show was an undercover friend of Matt's. And he'd see the Scream-O-Rama catch fire and call for back up. All that Matt needed to do was move Val and Sdenka's coffins to the Fortune Teller's store front, and they'd be free.

So, when the insomniac Val felt her coffin moving from its position in the basement of the Scream-O-Rama dark train ride, she felt as though she would finally be free. After so long, she would be free from the two who'd spent the better part of four hundred years making her regret surviving the Inquisitors burning her family in Zugarramurdi.

She and Sdenka and someday Matt would be able to live in peace without having to look over their shoulder because of bodies.

She waited for hours until she heard the second coffin get laid next to hers, and she smiled.

The smile died when she rose from the coffin, and next to her was the blonde who made her soul wail.

"Why are we here?" Asked Dolly.

"I—I—what?" Val looked around her, they weren't in the basement of the dark ride, they were next to her Fortune Teller's table. "Where is Sdenka?"

She smelled fresh blood and so did Dolly. Their fangs grew almost in unison as they looked toward the source of the smell.

In the far corner of the room, Detective Matthew Hopkins was propped against the wall, a long piece of metal impaled through his stomach and out of his back.

"Matt?" Val went to him and saw that he was still alive, if just barely. Taped to his chest was a piece of paper with the word "betrayer" scrawled on it.

"I didn't expect you to give me him." Said Dolly coming over to them. "But if the Count did all this, then I suppose he was a fighter. He'll do."

"Don't touch him." Val backhanded Dolly and she fell to the ground.

She was more shocked than anything.

"Have you forgotten your place, witch?"

"Fuck you, you spoiled brat. Our lives are fucked because of you, you absolute—"

Val's own voice interrupted her.

"Fire. We burned down Dreamland…"

Her conversation with Matt from the night before was playing back and filling the room.

"It's a trap, Val." Said Hopkins, weak from the loss of blood.

"I'll have you staked and left in the sun for you to burn when the Count returns, Valeria." Dolly's eyes turned entirely red, no whites or pupils. "If there is anything left."

"There won't be need for that." The voice cut through the air from all sides like a thousand knives. "I love man's ingenuity at times. And the microphone is no exception."

Val looked to the crystal ball and cursed at herself for being so stupid.

"I do applaud your plan, Valeria. Perhaps now, I will not be punished for the countess' specific tastes."

"Count, have I displeased you?" Dolly was sounding meek.

"You brought policemen close to my coffin far too often. This is your punishment."

Dolly ran for the door, but her hand flew back. The knob was red hot, and the smoke had started to come in through the cracks under the doors.

"Please, you cannot—"

"You presume to tell me what I can and cannot do, Countess?"

"I am your bride, Count." Dolly sounded like she was going to cry.

"I will find another."

"No!" Dolly screamed. It was cut short by part of the ceiling caving in on her.

Val broke one of the windows, but the fire was already overtaking every path of exit. Through the smoke, she could see Sdenka's red hair next to a man in black. They left through the crowd as the lights of police cars came near. Once again, the Third Bride would become First.

José Panbehchi is an attorney, horror fanatic, and cat enthusiast based out of New York City. Originally from Virginia, his relationship with Dracula began at an early age when his father would watch Hammer Horror movies in the other room. This is his first published story.

What You Have To Do To Keep Her

By Amelia Mangan

First of all, you have to get rid of everything red. In her room. All through the apartment. And everywhere. Raina's coming home this afternoon, Dad says, and everything red has to go, because it'll only remind her.

"What about these?" you say, holding up a pair of red platforms. "She loves these. She wore them to the winter formal."

Dad, stuffing a garbage bag, shakes his head. "It's just not good for her right now, Nika," he says, and holds out his hand. You'd hoped, someday, to wear these shoes. But you hand them over, watch them disappear into the bag.

Dad looks around, letting breath hiss through his teeth. Raina's posters have been ripped down, torn edges black on colorless paint. Her books went to Goodwill yesterday, except for the ones she liked when she was very young. Her makeup is in the trash—red nails, red lips, perfumes smelling of flowers and earth. Even her pink coverlet is gone, because you can't be too careful. Is what Dad says.

He looks at you. "Those sleeves are kinda short, don't you think?"

You look down. They've ridden up, exposing the crooks of your arms. You can see the thin blue rivers of your veins, right where the bones meet. "This is the longest shirt I've got."

"Maybe wear a sweater."

"It's warm."

"It's October."

"It's LA."

"Nika," Dad says, and stops. He's out of breath. Sweating. Staring at the wall, dark eyes big and blank like empty screens. He does this a lot lately. He used to do it more when you were little, and it scared you, because even though you didn't understand it, you knew it meant he wasn't with you, he wasn't really there.

You grab an armful of Raina's clothes and drop them into the bag. Dad blinks, looks at it.

"Should I get a new bag?" you say.

"It's fine, honey," he says. "What's the time?"

"Four-thirty-five."

"Four-thirty-five," Dad repeats. He moves to the window.

The street is mostly deserted. A few straggling kids, thin voices crying out as they dart for lengthening doorways. Crepe pumpkins, witches' hats. A latticed mesh of fire escapes. The sun hasn't set, but it's halfway below the distant mountains, and the minute it goes under the street will flood with darkness. It happens every evening. Sometimes it happens so fast you don't even notice.

"Should've had them bring her home earlier," Dad says. "Gonna be night soon. Oh God, and all the Halloween shit everywhere. *Christ.*"

He doesn't sound like he's talking to you—wouldn't be swearing if he was—so you shouldn't say anything. Keep quiet. Pay attention. It's important to pay attention, because that way you don't miss anything dangerous.

Dad gasps, pulls back. "She's *here!*"

You run to his side. A cab is out front, long hunchbacked silhouette on pale concrete. Movement inside and then she's out. Duffel bag over one shoulder. Sleeveless top. Dark hair chained in a French braid. Someone must've done that for her before she left the clinic.

She stands in the street as the cab pulls away. Her shadow is very tall.

You look to Dad. He's knotting his hands together, hard enough to make them tremble. "I should get down there," he says. "Say hi. Bring her up. Right?"

You didn't realize he was talking to you again. There you go, not paying attention. "Probably?" you say.

Dad nods, forcefully, like he's been given instructions, and turns to leave.

There's a knock at the front door.

Dad freezes. You freeze.

Three more knocks. Slow, deliberate. Sarcastic. "You gonna let me in or what?"

You don't know what you expected her to sound like, after everything. Maybe sort of spooky or hypnotized. But she just sounds like Raina.

Dad snaps out of whatever state he's in and hisses, "Nika. *Sweater.*"

You hurtle out of Raina's room, into yours. Grab a sweater, put it on.

Wear long sleeves. That's another thing you have to remember to do. For as long as she's here. For as long as she stays.

She'll stay. You'll make sure of it. You and Dad, together.

You enter the living room. Dad is beside the door, and your sister is back. Standing still, absorbing it all. Her nostrils flare, the tiniest bit.

She looks good. Healthy. Pale still, but there's a glow beneath the skin. A hot, coursing river of strangers' blood.

The clinic had to use five gallons. For the transfusion, to save her life, bring her back from the life that wasn't life. How many people in five gallons? About three.

Up close, you can see the black bruises all over her arms. The thick ropes of re-inflated veins. And the teeth marks. Dark vines, infected tattoos. Trailing from her wrists, up her forearms, all the way to her neck. They're worst on her neck.

As if sensing you looking, she twists that neck, catches you in a headlight stare. Her eyes are so bright. No hiding from them.

"Holy *shit!*" she whoops. Lets her bag fall. "Little baby sister!"

You have to understand she's *cured* now. Dad said so. The FBI people brought her into the clinic, after they'd set the compound on fire and pulled her out, and the clinic cured her. She won't hurt anyone anymore. She's herself again. She's so much herself, she's almost unrecognizable.

She holds out her bruised arms, full of other people's blood, and waits. "You gonna hug me?"

You move closer. Freeze up again.

Raina keeps on waiting.

Dad tries to save it. "It's a little soon, Raina."

"A little soon," repeats Raina. "Well. That makes sense."

She lowers her arms. Tucks them behind her back.

"Still. *Look* at you, kiddo! When'd you get so *tall?* You're, what, twelve now?"

"Eleven," you say. "Last month."

Shouldn't have said that. Shouldn't remind her how long it's been since she ran away.

"Aw, man," Raina says. Mild annoyance. Like she's misplaced something. "And I didn't even get you a present. Jeez. Am I an asshole or what?"

"It's okay," you say. "It wasn't a *big* birthday. There wasn't a party."

"I got her a cake," says Dad.

"He got you a cake?" says Raina. "Sounds like a party to me."

"It was very quiet," says Dad.

"The cake? Uh, yeah, Dad, food doesn't talk. Usually."

And she looks at you. And she *winks*.

"The *party*, Raina," says Dad. Pained.

"It wasn't a party," you say. "Really."

"Wish I could've been there. Nobody had parties at the clinic," says Raina. "Nobody got cake. There *was* a gift shop, though, which was weird. I guess it's so visiting parents can pretend like they thought to bring their kid something. Could've gotten you some flowers there. Though they probably would've died by the time I got here, huh."

"It's enough that you were thinking of her," says Dad. "Honestly."

"I wasn't, though," says Raina. "I was thinking of parties. I was thinking of cake."

Silence.

"It's good that you're hungry," you say. You regret it, instantly.

"Oh, wow, is it?" says Raina. "Is that good, Dad? Me being hungry? I wouldn't have thought that was good. Being hungry isn't good, right?"

"I can fix you something," Dad says. "Or order pizza. Or whatever you like."

"Mm. Whatever I like," says Raina. "It's actually hard to think of anything I like." She saunters to the couch. "You know what, ask me later. Been a long day. Maybe I'm tired."

"I'm sorry I didn't answer the door right away," Dad says. Very stiff. "Nika and I were cleaning up for you."

"Yeah? That was thoughtful," says Raina, collapsing onto the couch, throwing her feet up on the table.

"We wanted things to be nice for you. Clean. Comfortable."

"Well, you know how I like to be clean and comfortable," says Raina, picking up the remote. "Thank you, Daddy. Thank you, Nika."

Dad watches her. One arm is crossed over his body, grasping the crook of his elbow. "I really am sorry. About the door."

"It's fine. Not like I need to be invited in or anything." She turns the TV on. "Not anymore."

And, before Dad can respond: "So, Nika, what'd I miss on *Days*? Is Marlena still possessed or what?"

Sit in the armchair. It's a good distance. Far enough away, but also pretty close.

Maybe you should've hugged her after all.

There was a Halloween long before this one. You barely remember it. It probably doesn't matter, but you find yourself thinking of it, even though you shouldn't.

You were little. You don't really remember what it was like, being little, but you do remember Mom had left by then, so you must've been five or six. You were in the street, walking behind Raina. She could only have been about eleven herself, but her legs seemed so much longer than yours. Never looked back, even when you called her name. She wore a glittery scarf, covering her mouth, but her gaze was fixed under angry black brows, and breath came out of her nose in hot, hard snorts. The scarf rippled when she breathed, and even though it was dark and the mountains blocked the stars, you could see the glitter shimmering like light on water.

A burning smell. Ash specks on dark air. Maybe there were bonfires that night. Or maybe the hills were on fire again.

Raina was holding a cat. A sandy-blonde kitten, clutched against her chest. *Was the cat ours?* You can't remember. It bothers you, the not-remembering. *Did we ever have a cat?*

Dad wasn't there. Dad was nowhere. Dad was sick then. He'd gone to get some medicine, he said, but he hadn't been home in four days. *Let's go Trick-or-Treating*, Raina said. *I know he said he'd take us. But fuck it. Let's go without him.*

Raina was so angry. *So* angry. Sometimes it looked like she might be crying. Maybe it was just the glitter.
The cat was crying, too. Pressed against Raina's heart. She was squeezing it so tight.

You don't remember what happened to the cat. Much later, after Dad started going to his meetings and things were sort of better, you told him about going Trick-or-Treating, and about the cat.

Dad sat there a long time. He took your hands. Pressed them between his own. "You understand," he said, "that Raina is just really mad, right? She doesn't mean the things she does."

"Okay."

"And she's mad at *me*. Not you. None of this is your fault. You need to understand that."

"Okay."

He went quiet again. "The part about the cat. That was only a dream. A bad dream, from a bad time. Don't worry about that. Or any of it. Okay?"

"Okay."

"Okay," said Dad, and squeezed your hands tight.

Do not think about what might've happened to the cat.

Dinner is vegetarian. All dinners, from now on, have to be vegetarian.

You lay out plates. Dad takes the casserole from the oven. Raina watches. She's seen her room by now. Dad hovered in the doorway while she took it all in. A long time passed and then she said: "Looks good." And that was all.

Dad took her door off its hinges. It's leaning in the hallway. She didn't mention it.

You sit. Dad serves Raina first. She looks at her plate. "Yummy," she says.

Dad smiles. Nervous.

"Been a while since I had this," Raina says. "A good old-fashioned home-cooked meal. Boy, did I miss it."

She doesn't touch it.

"Is it too hot?" asks Dad.

"Yeah," Raina allows. "Maybe that's it."

She looks at you. Her stare is still so bright, but her voice, when she speaks, is softer. "*You* should eat, though, Nika."

You're not hungry, and Dad's cooking is never good. But you eat.

"How is it?" Raina asks.

"Good."

Dad almost beams.

"Ratdaddy always made sure we ate first," Raina says. "That wasn't his *name* or anything. I couldn't pronounce that. He was European. Born a *super* long time ago. But he didn't like me using his name anyway. Or talking at all."

Dad goes still.

"Tara was the one who said to call him Ratdaddy," Raina goes on. "Not to his face, obviously. Just to have something to call him. He *looked* like a rat. Black eyes. Sharp teeth."

Dad coughs. "I don't—"

"Tara—I dunno if her real name was Tara? She was the oldest," Raina says. "Of the three of us. There was Tara and me and … God, what was her name? Doesn't matter. But she was the only blonde. This pale, pale blonde. Hair like little wisps of smoke. Tara and me, we were both so dark, and so much taller than her. When we all stood together, like *surrounding* someone? On some of the night raids Ratdaddy took us on, in those desert towns? Oh my God. We looked *so* cool."

Dad laughs, without managing to smile. "This, this really is *not* appropriate dinner conversation, ladies. Nika, how was sch–"

"Of course, we couldn't *see* ourselves," Raina keeps going. "Not in mirrors and stuff. So we had to ask each other how we looked, all the time. It was hilarious. Couldn't ask Ratdaddy, of course. Couldn't *ask* Ratdaddy anything. But he gave us everything we needed."

"Raina," Dad says.

"The blonde, she was about your age," Raina says to you, "so she was really little. Never ate enough. Ratdaddy brought things back for her. Little things. Animals. And other little things. But she just never ate enough. Played with her food, y'know? Like a cat. Like a kitten."

The food lodges in your throat. It sticks there, greasy and burning. Dad's hand clenches around his fork.

"Anyway, doesn't matter," says Raina. "I'm cured and they all burned to death." She picks up her fork, digs in. "Mm," she says. "Yummy."

It's late. Dad is in the kitchen. Dad is on the phone, trying to keep his voice down. Dad thinks you've gone to bed.

You can't hear who's on the phone from out in the hall, but you're pretty sure it's Mike, Dad's sponsor. You asked Raina once, not long before she left, what a sponsor was. "Somebody who tells you you're not the piece of shit you know you are," was all she said.

"It was too soon," Dad says. "I *knew* that. But I thought it'd be better. Being home was better for me. I know it's not the same thing, but…"

Pause.

"I don't think so. They wouldn't take her back, and even if they would, our insurance won't cover it."

He puts a hand over his eyes. "Oh God, Mike, I wanna get out. She's only been home a day and it feels like I've been trapped in this apartment forever. I just wanna go get high so fucking *bad*."

Pause.

"Nah. Thanks, though."

Pause.

"Yeah, maybe." An edge in his voice. "But I don't *want* to."

Pause, and Dad smacks the tabletop. You jump. He doesn't see it.

"Because I don't fucking *believe* it anymore, okay? I just *don't*."

Pause. A sigh.

"Okay. Okay, yes. Fine." He screws his eyes shut, pinches the flesh between them. "*God grant me the serenity to accept the things I cannot change…*"

Mike is saying it at the same time, like always, so this is your moment to move away. Dad can't hear you now.

You have to pass Raina's room to get to yours. Can't avoid it. As you move toward the black square of her doorway you see her. She is sitting on the edge of the bed, back straight, shoulders arched. She is staring into the darkness.

The door is almost behind you. You risk a glance back.

The viewpoint is different now, the angle changed. You see that Raina's stare is directed not into nothingness, but into the mirror on her closet door.

Very slow, she raises her hand, palm outwards. The mirror—Raina copies her.

She flexes her fingers. A wave at an almost-stranger. Someone nearly forgotten.

The double does likewise.

The mangled arm bends. Her fingertips trail up her ripped, gashed neck. The ragged moons of her nails dent the curving skin.

Her face is soft and expressionless. A sleepwalker's mask.

You go to bed. You think you won't sleep tonight; you think you won't dream, but you do. It's just that when you wake, you'll never remember it.

Raina is not allowed out. Ever.

Dad locks the doors before he goes to work. The windows, too. You're allowed to go to and from school, nowhere else. You are not to give Raina your key.

Dad's staying out later. More meetings, probably. There have been times when he went to three meetings a day, all week long. That was back when things were really bad.

A lot of the time, you're alone. Raina stays in her room. You keep to the living room mostly. Vacuum the rug. Wash dishes. Stay useful.

The days pass. The planet turns.

One morning you wake up early. Slouch through the faded light, into the hall.

Has Dad come home? He has. In his room, blanket over his head. Relief washes into you, and for a moment you get to enjoy that feeling of rightness, of safety. But then you remember you have to check on Raina, and the feeling curdles in your belly. You creep toward Raina's doorway. Pull in breath, peer around the frame.

Raina isn't there.

The world is lit by lightning-strike panic. *Raina isn't there.* Nothing else registers—not the fact that the street sounds are louder, not the cool dawn air flowing from the open fire escape, nothing. You let out the breath and as it leaves your throat you sag, you swoon. This is relief of a sort, too.

The sounds return. Distant traffic. Waking birds. The rush of the wind. And the rhythmic thud of boots on metal. Raina always swung her legs whenever she was restless—at the dentist's, at the child psychiatrist's, whatever. Drove Dad crazy.

Follow the sound. She's sitting on the fire escape, legs dangling through the ironwork. Staring out at the street. Staring out *of* the street. Past the lamps, winking out one at a time; past the cars crawling the highways beyond. Staring up into the mountains.

Don't ask how she got out here. Don't ask why she's wearing shoes. Don't ask anything. You could probably sneak away.

"You know why people don't go jogging in LA after dark, Nika?" Raina says, without turning.

You don't answer. You don't know.

"After dark," Raina says, "wild things come down from the mountains. There are mountains all around this town, did you know that? They have us surrounded. And there are so many wild things roaming the tops of those mountains. Wolves, coyotes. Big cats. *Huge.* And as soon as the sun comes down, they come down too, and they walk the streets, all over the city. It was theirs before it was ever ours. And if they see anybody running, they'll follow them. Miles and miles. Until you drop, and that's when they have you."

You move closer. You shouldn't, but you do.

"People didn't go out after dark where I lived, either. Near the compound. Same reason. They were afraid. For a while I didn't know whether or not I liked that people were afraid. Eventually I decided I did."

She looks at you. Smiles. When she smiles, you can see where they filed down her eyeteeth.

"One day everything will die," says Raina. "Everything human. And when that happens, when the last person is gone and everything's over, that's when the wild things will rule. All the big cats will come down from the mountains and this time they'll stay. Everything will be theirs again, like it was before. It'll happen so fast, Nika. You'll never believe it, how fast it'll happen."

You look at her. For the first time, you don't look away.

She does, though. Her eyes slip from you, back into the distance. The sun is coming up. It isn't here yet, but its light has almost reached you.

Halloween Night.

No decorations. No witches, no monsters, no bats. No candy. Dad has taped a sign to the door: "NO TRICK-OR-TREATERS THANK YOU."

"So we won't be bothered," he explains. Smiles brightly. "But that doesn't mean we can't have fun, right? We can watch a movie. I bought popcorn."

"Fun," is all Raina says.

You're all together on the couch. Dad on the far end, leaning against the arm in a way he thinks doesn't look like he's watching you both. You on the other end, unsure how to arrange your limbs. Raina in the middle. You can hear her boots kicking at the bottom of the couch.

Dad turns the TV on, and you immediately understand this was a mistake, because it's Halloween Night and so the image flashing up onscreen is of a white-faced man with brilliant black hair wrapping a wilting girl in his cloak, sinking doglike teeth into her neck. Violins shriek as blood, too red to be real, courses down the arch of her throat.

Dad fumbles for the remote, hissing "*Fuck*" through gritted teeth. Raina's spine has gone very straight.

Dad switches channels and now the screen just shows local news.

Quiet. The anchors laugh about something. The sound is too low to hear what.

"It's not like that, you know," Raina says.

"Oh, Jesus," you hear Dad mutter.

"People don't just stand there. Let you do it to them. You have to, like, *persuade* them. That's why it took three of us," Raina goes on. "Sometimes you'd get someone big, and it'd be harder to persuade them on your own. All the yelling and thrashing and stuff. Sometimes it was fun. Like a mechanical bull or something."

"Raina," says Dad.

"And you don't just chomp someone's neck like that. I didn't even *use* my teeth for that part." She examines her fingernails. Still ragged, but you see now they're long, and sharp.

"Ratdaddy made us persuade people for him. He was old. We had to hold them down." She looks at her hands again. Her voice is neutral. "*He* used his teeth. All the time."

"*Raina*," says Dad, "I don't like you talking about this. Okay? Let's talk about something else."

"Why?" says Raina. Very calm. "Why can't I talk about it? Don't they say at your meetings it's better to talk?"

"*Stop* it," Dad says. "I want this to stop. Right now, okay? You're scaring your sister."

"Am I, Nika? Are you the one I'm scaring?"

"No," you say. Adjust your voice. It's too high. "But I think actually there's some dishes still. From dinner. I'll wash them, okay, Dad?"

Head for the kitchen. Turn the water up loud. Make sure it's hot enough that you can plunge your hands in and not think about anything else.

Wash a dish. Put it in the cabinet. Another one. Another.

"Hey."

Raina leans in the doorway.

"Was he right? Were you scared?"

You shake your head.

Raina straightens. Hesitates. Crosses to the sink, near you, not too near. She picks up a washcloth, turns it over.

"I talk too much," she says. "I hear myself. At the compound, none of us talked for days sometimes. Weeks, even." She plucks a dish from the rack, rubs the cloth over it.

"I just wanted you to hear me," she says.

Take the dish and put it in the cabinet. That's what you move in closer to do, only that, but she's there, and she's Raina, and she's been gone so long. Your arms are around her back and your face is buried in her shirt. She stiffens, and then she bends, enfolds you. The torn skin of her arm is rough and cool against your cheek. The muscles beneath are strong.

"Nika?" Dad's voice wavers in the dark. You open your eyes and there he is, over Raina's shoulder. His face is so white. He looks more like the guy in the movie than Raina ever could. "Sweetheart? Come back inside now. I think the dishes are as clean as they're ever gonna be." He tries to smile.

Raina looks at him. *Stares* at him. Something twists under the skin of her face.

"You think I would," she says. Very flat. Very quiet. "You *believe* that."

She straightens. Her hands rest on your shoulders.

Dad steps forward. Stops. "Let's all go back inside."

"I'm fine here," says Raina. The thinnest edges of her nails move up the side of your neck. You can feel your pulse vibrating against her fingertips.

Dad swallows. "Nika. C'mere a minute, okay, honey? I wanna talk to you."

"You got something to tell her? Tell *me*," says Raina. "I wanna hear it, too."

Dad can't speak.

Raina's lip twitches. She slides her hands down your back, gives you a gentle push.

A couple of strides and she's in front of Dad. Looking at him. He looks back, just.

Raina lunges, teeth bared, fingers hooked into claws. Dad flinches back.

She stares. Laughs a little. It doesn't sound like she thinks anything's funny.

As she passes, you hear her murmur in his ear: "If I wanted to, y'know? If I actually fucking *cared*."

And she's out. Her footsteps track, unhurried, into her room. You and Dad are left behind.

You're still holding the dish. You move to put it away.

"*Leave* it!" Dad screams.

You freeze.

Dad holds his arm across his body, trying to stop the trembling. He looks at you, breathing like it hurts.

He turns. Leaves you.

Wait until his bedroom door closes. Put the dish away.

S omething wakes you in the night. No sound that you remember. Just some feeling, some kind of pull inside. You get up. Head for the kitchen.

There's light coming in, from the window, from the moon, but not enough, not nearly enough. Raina is crouched on the table. You can't see her face, but her hands are raised to her mouth, and you can hear something being eaten, something wet.

Through the moonbeams you see liquid spilling out of her, from between her legs. It hits the tablecloth, makes a sound like rain on a roof. You can't tell if she's peeing or bleeding. In the dark, everything that comes from a body looks black.

Raina's head turns. You still can't see her face. It's a shadow on a wall, no depth to it, no substance.

She speaks. Soft. "This isn't happening, kiddo. It's only a dream."

She slithers from the tabletop. Faceless, formless. Her hands cup your face. Her palms, her nails, are wet.

"I'm not even here," she whispers. "I'm at the top of the mountain."

Next morning, you come back into the kitchen. Everything looks different, and the same. Dad is sitting at the table. The tablecloth has vanished.

Dad's phone is in front of him, just out of reach. He makes no move for it.

You know. But you have to ask. "Where's Raina?"

"She's gone."

And neither of you say anything.

"Did she leave a note?" you ask, eventually.

He shakes his head.

"Should we call the police?"

"It wouldn't do any good."

He doesn't move. Barely breathes.

"Did I fail?" you ask.

He lifts his eyes. He has that look, the not-here look, or it has him. "No, honey," he says. Very, very calm. "*You* didn't fail. Not *you*."

The words should make you feel better, even if the way he says them isn't right. You try to feel better. But you can't feel anything at all.

N ighttime now. All the lights are off. All the world is quiet.

Dad is gone. Said he was going to a meeting, but that was last night. Hasn't been home since. Left his phone behind. You're hungry, but there isn't any food in the fridge, and when you looked for money to order some, there was nothing. He'd taken it all.

You head down the hall. Past Raina's doorway. No need to look there now.

The fire escape is open. How long has it been open? Doesn't matter. Out on the fire escape and breathing, breathing. The air is different here. There's a taste at the back of your throat, gritty and biting, like ashes or dust, and it almost feels good and it almost hurts. But you can breathe through it, because you have to.

You're not supposed to go out alone after dark. Even Raina never wanted you to go out alone. But your feet are on the steps, and the metal cuts into your soles, forcing you down faster and faster, until you hit the ground.

The street is empty. Patches of lamplight streak the pavement, dapple the blackness. A mist covers the ground: the day's heat, risen from the stone.

No movement but your feet. No sound but your breath. There is no one out here. It's hard to remember there ever was.

Motion. Beneath a streetlamp, to your left. A flow of muscle. Pale hair and glowing eye.

You stand still. One hand pressed against your heart.

The mountain lion stops, sniffs the burning air. It twists its sandy-blonde head on its long, scarred neck until it sees you. Stares at you.

You stare back.

The night deepens. Great valleys, greater peaks. Cliffs and canyons.

The cat gives a languid blink. Golden eyes, liquid fire. They burn inside you a moment longer before it turns away, pads off silent into the dark.

Do not run after it. Do not give chase. This will follow you forever if you let it. It will hunt you down and eat your heart. There is nothing more to see within that golden stare, nothing left to find, nothing you want to find you.

There is only so much you can understand and hope to keep on living.

Amelia Mangan is an author currently living in Sydney, Australia. Her stories have been featured in a number of publications, including Dracula Beyond Stoker Volume 2 and The Best Horror of the Year Volume 11, and adapted in audio form by Jason Hill for the hit podcast Chilling Tales for Dark Nights. Her first novel, Release, was published by Nightscape Press in 2015.

THE COUNTESS

Countess Dolingen:
The Forgotten Bride of the StokerVerse
By Chris McAuley

A comprehensive exploration of female vampires in nineteenth century literature would be insufficient without acknowledging "Dracula's Guest," despite its publication in the twentieth century. This tale made its debut in *Dracula's Guest and Other Weird Stories*, a collection of posthumously published tales by Bram Stoker in 1914. In the preface, Florence Stoker, the author's widow, disclosed that her late husband had initially penned "Dracula's Guest" in the 1890's, as a segment of the larger work, *Dracula*.

"A few months before the lamented death of my husband—I might say even as the shadow of death was over him—he planned three series of short stories for publication, and the present volume is one of them. To his original list of stories in this book, I have added a hitherto unpublished episode from "Dracula." It was originally excised owing to the length of the book and may prove of interest to the many readers of what is considered my husband's most remarkable work.

The other stories have already been published in English and American periodicals. Had my husband lived longer, he might have seen fit to revise this work, which is mainly from the earlier years of his strenuous life. But as fate has entrusted to me the issuing of it, I consider it fitting and proper to let it go forth practically as it was left by him."
—Florence Stoker, Preface to Dracula's Guest

Dracula's Guest begins with an unnamed Englishman setting out by carriage from Munich. Dracula scholars Robert Eighteen-Bisang and Elizabeth Millar have provided evidence in their annotated facsimile of Stoker's notes that this character is indeed Jonathan Harker. As the story progresses Harker's journey is halted by Johann, his superstitious coachman. The deadly Walpurgis Night is upon them and all the denizens of Hell are about to break loose upon the earthly plane. Johann stops his coach at a mysterious crossroads, a location associated with the burial of those who have died by suicide. Johann explains to Harker why the Englishman must not explore the branch of the crossroads which leads to the graveyard.

"He (The coachman) burst out into a long story in German and English, so mixed up that I could not quite understand exactly what he said, but roughly I gathered that long ago, hundreds of years, men had died there and been buried in their graves; and sounds were heard under the clay, and when the graves were opened, men and women were found rosy with life, and their mouths red with blood. And so, in haste to save their lives (aye, and their souls!—and here he crossed himself) those who were left fled away to other places, where the living lived, and the dead were dead and not—not something. He was evidently afraid to speak the last words."
—Dracula's Guest

Of course, our plucky protagonist refuses to listen and hops off the coach to travel towards the abandoned village and graveyard by foot. We get our first, fleeting glimpse of Dracula as Johnathan glances back to see the coachman's horses startled by a tall, thin man who appears over a nearby hill. But Dracula isn't the main character or antagonist of this story. As Harker reaches the cemetery, he discovers a vast marble tomb. An epitaph in German reveals the name of the occupant—Countess Dolingen of Graz in Styria. He also discovers an epitaph from Gottfried August Burger's *Lenore*—"The dead travel fast"—and the cause of this noble lady's death is stated as seeking and finding it. Most tellingly a large iron spike (or perhaps stake) protrudes from the top of the tomb. It appears to have been driven inside!

It is not long before our hero meets this dead woman as a bolt of lightning strikes the iron spike while he foolishly takes shelter inside the tomb to evade a terrible storm.

> *"Just then there came another blinding flash, which seemed to strike the iron stake that surmounted the tomb and to pour through to the earth, blasting and crumbling the marble, as in a burst of flame. The dead woman rose for a moment of agony, while she was lapped in the flame, and her bitter scream of pain was drowned in the thundercrash."*
>
> —Dracula's Guest

After this, Haker loses consciousness and awakens to find a gigantic wolf licking at his throat. A troop of horsemen drive the creature away and there is a hint that this is no ordinary wolf as one of the soldiers' remarks that there is no point in pursuing it. Chillingly he also adds that only the sacred (silver) bullet, which they do not have, could injure or kill the beast.

Finally, back in the safety of Munich, Harker learns that the cause of his salvation was the owner of his hotel, who sent out a search party for him after receiving a telegram warning from a particular aristocrat:

> *"Bistritz.*

> *Be careful of my guest—his safety is most precious to me. Should aught happen to him, or if he be missed, spare nothing to find him and ensure his safety. He is English and therefore adventurous. There are often dangers from snow and wolves and night. Lose not a moment if you suspect harm to him. I answer your zeal with my fortune.—Dracula."*
>
> —Dracula's Guest

So, who was this mysterious woman and what exactly is her connection to Dracula? Bram Stoker's typescript features lines that have been removed from the final draft of the novel. These are lines which clearly relate to events from "Dracula's Guest." Harker recounts an unsettling experience of having his throat licked by a wolf and later shares with Dracula an incident in Munich involving the arrival of soldiers. Also, and most importantly, there is an omitted passage which relates to the famous encounter Harker has with the three female vampires (weird sisters/brides).

> *"It suddenly dawned on me that she was the woman— or her image—that I saw in the tomb on Walpurgis Night"*
>
> —Dracula Typescript

A vestige of this connection persists even in the published version of Dracula, where Harker finds one of the three women oddly familiar.

> *"I somehow recognized her face, associated with a haunting from some dream, but in that moment, I couldn't recall the specifics of when or where."*
>
> —Dracula

The figure of Countess Dolingen adds a layer of mystery to the broader narrative of Bram Stoker's novel. While the deleted passages from the typescript hint at the countess being one of the three female vampires encountered by Jonathan Harker, the extent of her connection to Dracula remains intriguingly ambiguous. The eerie circumstances surrounding her tomb, create a chilling atmosphere.

As Dacre Stoker and I delved deeper into this mystery we adopted the countess as a forgotten bride and through The StokerVerse accentuated the elements which intertwine her character with the supernatural elements that define the world of "Dracula".

There are also connections with J. Sheridan Le Fanu's 'Carmilla'. The abandoned village only inhabited by vampires as well as Dolingen's connection to Styria show's a tip of Bram Stoker's hat to the other literary masterpiece which came a few decades before.

Although not explicitly confirmed, the lingering echoes of her association with Harker's encounter with the brides leave a powerful impression on the tapestry of Stoker's gothic universe. Countess Dolingen remains a captivating enigma, a spectral figure whose significance resonates beyond the confines of her tomb, hinting at untold connections in the shadows of Dracula's realm.

Chris McAuley is a writer who specializes in the Horror, Science Fiction, Fantasy, Western, and Crime genres. He is the co-creator of the popular StokerVerse, along with Bram Stoker's great-grandnephew Dacre Stoker. He is also the co-creator of a science fiction and fantasy franchise with Babylon 5's Claudia Christian called Dark Legacies. He is the lead writer on the latest Astroboy animated tv show. Chris is also currently working on The Terminator film and game series, Star Trek and the Doctor Who franchise. Chris's work can be seen at www.dark-universes.com

For more information on the StokerVerse and to learn more about the products available visit www.stokerverse.com.

The Wedding Guest:
Marrying Dracula's Brides to Dracula's Guest
By Toothpickings

Dorothy Tree, Geraldine Dvorak, and Cornelia Thaw as Dracula's Brides
Dracula Universal Pictures 1931

Dracula's Brides have captured readers' imaginations for years, possibly because so little of their background is given. We are left to scratch out clues based on a handful of lines in the novel. If only there was some corroborating storylines, or some apocryphal sources we could consult to get a little more insight. Perhaps a prequel? Something commercial but with lots of fan service.

Something modeled on Star Wars: Rogue One.

We don't have to think outside the casket on this one. Bram Stoker already provided his own Rogue One, published after his death by his widow, Florence Stoker: the short story "Dracula's Guest".

Originally cast as an excised chapter by Florence Stoker, "Dracula's Guest" weaves the tale of an unnamed Englishman as he spends a harrowing Walpurgis Night dodging ghoulish beings. Notably, it's not told in the epistolary manner that Dracula would take, suggesting that the story was written early enough in Stoker's process that he hadn't yet adopted the letter-writing, found footage style that would eventually characterize his longer novel.

Despite misleading titles and credits, it's never been dramatized in big-budget films[1]; and seldom adapted even by independent storytellers[2]. Which is a missed opportunity, because like targeting womprat-sized exhaust vents, it would be explosive.

What "Dracula's Guest" gives us isn't a welcoming Count who offers spice tea and games of holochess. In fact, Dracula the character never physically appears in "Dracula's Guest"; there's barely anything to connect the story to the Count until the last few lines. Hey, that's sort of like the ending of Rogue One when all those familiar faces show up. Analogies are fun!

But who does appear is Countess Dolingen, a bloodthirsty being that nearly takes the life of our Englishman inside a tomb on Walpurgis Night, before eventually being taken down by a wolf. Think of Countess Dolingen as a sexier Cruella Deville and the wolf as a dalmatian that will eat your face.

The events of "Dracula's Guest" leave a lot of room for interpretation. And boy how gothic scholars have delivered! If you think George Lucas stans have a Boba Fettish for deleted scenes and early drafts, get a load of the all the fan theories connecting

---

[1] Both 1936's *Dracula's Daughter* and 2008's *Dracula's Guest* claim to be based upon Stoker's story, but bear little resemblance.

[2] One notable exception is Eternity Comics' 1991 *Dracula: The Lady in the Tomb* written by DBS contributor Steven Philip Jones, with art by Robert Schnieders.

"Dracula's Guest" to Dracula. Most of these involve the young Englishman being either Jonathan Harker—very reasonable—or Renfield—a stretch but tantalizing—or some earlier victim sent long before Harker—possible, but honestly kind of dull.

But the more intriguing theory surrounds Countess Dolingen, and the idea that she is one of the Brides. This is supported by research Leslie Klinger did into Stoker's manuscript of Dracula, where Harker observes that one of the Brides reminds him of the Countess "seen in the tomb of Walpurgis Night." This would make Dolingen the only Bride with a name—not quite acing the Transylvanian Bechtel Test but inching a step closer.

The case against this connection is that the woman of "Dracula's Guest" appears to be an independent actor, who has her own abode in the Romanian countryside where she separates wayward travelers from their lives. That doesn't quite square with Dracula, where she is subsumed into the bridal trio, presumably is confined to the castle, and never so much as gets a name.

So there's a lot of room for interpretation. Unfortunately, representations of Countess Dolingen in popular media are uncommon. I can't think of a single major film, comic, or show that portrayed her by name. Sure, the 1981 French film "The Crimes of Countess Dolingen" had a promising title, but it wasn't what we'd hope for.

However, there may be one marvelous exception to this oversight. And it's a century-old Easter Egg that's been hiding in plain sight.

Tod Browning's 1931 Dracula made a number of compromises to adapt a book to screen by way of a stage play. One is reimagining Jonathan Harker's journey into Transylvania as Renfield's, so in order to have a conversation straddling the book, short story, and the 1931 film, I'll refer to the character as Harker/Renfield.

(Other changes in the film include making Seward a father to Mina instead of a suitor, and including 100% more armadillos than were found in the book.)

But amongst all the changes, perhaps Browning and his creative team found a way to wink at the audience, a way to say "We stand atop MY achievement!"

That key moment comes early in the film. When Harker/Renfield arrives at an inn in Transylvania, there's an uncredited, but featured, performance by a young woman who stares at Harker/Renfield from a window. She stares intensely—we might even say hungrily—at the traveling Englishman.

And in case we thought this was just a weird performance aberration, Tod Browning's camera cuts back to her a second time so she can close the window on Harker/Renfield, slowly and deliberately. The intense stare is still there, stark and unflinching.

Was this seemingly random appearance by Dorothy Tree a nod to "Dracula's Guest?"
Dracula Universal Pictures 1931

One sharp eyed fan—Melvyn M. Sobel—noticed that this uncredited woman staring at Renfield with mysterious intensity looked a lot—an awful lot—like actress Dorothy Tree. And who else did Dorothy Tree play? She played one of The Brides later in the same film. In case we missed it, she also plays a Bride in the Spanish language Drácula.

It would appear that we have a Bride of Dracula watching Harker/Renfield hungrily, threateningly, from a village window. Perhaps she has been stalking him all along this journey. Perhaps she had her own plans for him. Perhaps she was Countess Dolingen.

If we read "Dracula's Guest" as being in the same universe as Dracula despite minor inconsistencies, Dolingen is the only vampire besides Dracula that leaves the castle. Casting one of the same actors from the bridal pageant as a villager with menace in her eyes may be the very tip-of-the-hat that Browning felt Dracula needed to connect it to "Dracula's Guest".

Would Dorothy Tree be able to shed any light on this question? Unfortunately, no. She was blacklisted by the House Unamerican Activities Committee later in her career—possibly in retaliation for vocalizing opposition to HUAC years before. Like her costar Bela Lugosi, who fled his own home country due to political persecution, Dorothy Tree would live in relative obscurity after her biggest roles had passed.

But if we are wrong—if the Countess Dolingen of the crypt on Walpurgis Night was not one of the Brides of Dracula—then perhaps she is still out there. Perhaps somewhere in the Transylvanian countryside there's a tomb waiting for traveler to take shelter from the storm, and that traveler will not have the benefit of a supernatural wolf to scare away whatever lurks inside. That's a blockbuster sequel I'd buy a ticket for.

Toothpickings, the gothic double of **Brian Forrest**, shapeshifts between written blogs and YouTube videos while metering traffic at the crossroads of vampire folklore, fiction, and pop culture. Toothpickings is currently working on a documentary on *Blacula* director William Crain. To find Toothpickings before the next sunrise, try Twitter or the nearest plot of native soil.

Dracula's Guest
By Bram Stoker

When we started for our drive the sun was shining brightly on Munich, and the air was full of the joyousness of early summer. Just as we were about to depart, Herr Delbrück (the maître d'hôtel of the Quatre Saisons, where I was staying) came down, bareheaded, to the carriage and, after wishing me a pleasant drive, said to the coachman, still holding his hand on the handle of the carriage door:

"Remember you are back by nightfall. The sky looks bright but there is a shiver in the north wind that says there may be a sudden storm. But I am sure you will not be late." Here he smiled, and added, "for you know what night it is."

Johann answered with an emphatic, "Ja, mein Herr," and, touching his hat, drove off quickly. When we had cleared the town, I said, after signalling to him to stop:

"Tell me, Johann, what is tonight?"

He crossed himself, as he answered laconically: "Walpurgis nacht." Then he took out his watch, a great, old-fashioned German silver thing as big as a turnip, and looked at it, with his eyebrows gathered together and a little impatient shrug of his shoulders. I realised that this was his way of respectfully protesting against the unnecessary delay, and sank back in the carriage, merely motioning him to proceed. He started off rapidly, as if to make up for lost time. Every now and then the horses seemed to throw up their heads and sniffed the air suspiciously. On such occasions I often looked round in alarm. The road was pretty bleak, for we were traversing a sort of high, wind-swept plateau. As we drove, I saw a road that looked but little used, and which seemed to dip through a little, winding valley. It looked so inviting that, even at the risk of offending him, I called Johann to stop —and when he had pulled up, I told him I would like to drive down that road. He made all sorts of excuses, and frequently crossed himself as he spoke. This somewhat piqued my curiosity, so I asked him various questions. He answered fencingly, and repeatedly looked at his watch in protest. Finally I said:

"Well, Johann, I want to go down this road. I shall not ask you to come unless you like; but tell me why you do not like to go, that is all I ask." For answer he seemed to throw himself off the box, so quickly did he reach the ground. Then he stretched out his hands appealingly to me, and implored me not to go. There was just enough of English mixed with the German for me to understand the drift of his talk. He seemed always just about to tell me something—the very idea of which evidently frightened him; but each time he pulled himself up, saying, as he crossed himself: "Walpurgis-Nacht!"

I tried to argue with him, but it was difficult to argue with a man when I did not know his language. The advantage certainly rested with him, for although he began to speak in English, of a very crude and broken kind, he always got excited and broke into his native tongue—and every time he did so, he looked at his watch. Then the horses became restless and sniffed the air. At this he grew very pale, and, looking around in a frightened way, he suddenly jumped forward, took them by the bridles and led them on some twenty feet. I followed, and asked why he had done this. For answer he crossed himself, pointed to the spot we had left and drew his carriage in the direction of the other road, indicating a cross, and said, first in German, then in English: "Buried him—him what killed themselves."

I remembered the old custom of burying suicides at cross-roads: "Ah! I see, a suicide. How interesting!" But for the life of me I could not make out why the horses were frightened.

Whilst we were talking, we heard a sort of sound between a yelp and a bark. It was far away; but the horses got very restless, and it took Johann all his time to quiet them. He was pale, and said, "It sounds like a wolf—but yet there are no wolves here now."

"No?" I said, questioning him; "isn't it long since the wolves were so near the city?"

"Long, long," he answered, "in the spring and summer; but with the snow the wolves have been here not so long."

Whilst he was petting the horses and trying to quiet them, dark clouds drifted rapidly across the sky. The sunshine passed away, and a breath of cold wind seemed to drift past us. It was only a breath, however, and more in the nature of a warning than a fact, for the sun came out brightly again. Johann looked under his lifted hand at the horizon and said:

"The storm of snow, he comes before long time." Then he looked at his watch again, and, straightway holding his reins firmly—for the horses were still pawing the ground restlessly and shaking their heads—he climbed to his box as though the time had come for proceeding on our journey.

I felt a little obstinate and did not at once get into the carriage.

"Tell me," I said, "about this place where the road leads," and I pointed down.

Again he crossed himself and mumbled a prayer, before he answered, "It is unholy."

"What is unholy?" I enquired.

"The village."

"Then there is a village?"

"No, no. No one lives there hundreds of years." My curiosity was piqued, "But you said there was a village."

"There was."

"Where is it now?"

Whereupon he burst out into a long story in German and English, so mixed up that I could not quite understand exactly what he said, but roughly I gathered that long ago, hundreds of years, men had died there and been buried in their graves; and sounds were heard under the clay, and when the graves were opened, men and women were found rosy with life, and their mouths red with blood. And so, in haste to save their lives (aye, and their souls!—and here he crossed himself) those who were left fled away to other places, where the living lived, and the dead were dead and not—not something. He was evidently afraid to speak the last words. As he proceeded with his narration, he grew more and more excited. It seemed as if his imagination had got hold of him, and he ended in a perfect paroxysm of fear—white-faced, perspiring, trembling and looking round him, as if expecting that some dreadful presence would manifest itself there in the bright sunshine on the open plain. Finally, in an agony of desperation, he cried:

"Walpurgis nacht!" and pointed to the carriage for me to get in. All my English blood rose at this, and, standing back, I said:

"You are afraid, Johann—you are afraid. Go home; I shall return alone; the walk will do me good." The carriage door was open. I took from the seat my oak walking-stick—which I always carry on my holiday excursions—and closed the door, pointing back to Munich, and said, "Go home, Johann—Walpurgis-nacht doesn't concern Englishmen."

The horses were now more restive than ever, and Johann was trying to hold them in, while excitedly imploring me not to do anything so foolish. I pitied the poor fellow, he was deeply in earnest; but all the same I could not help laughing. His English was quite gone now. In his anxiety he had forgotten that his only means of making me understand was to talk my language, so he jabbered away in his native German. It began to be a little tedious. After giving the direction, "Home!" I turned to go down the cross-road into the valley.

With a despairing gesture, Johann turned his horses towards Munich. I leaned on my stick and looked after him. He went slowly along the road for a while: then there came over the crest of the hill a man tall and thin. I could see so much in the distance. When he drew near the horses, they began to jump and kick about, then to scream with terror. Johann could not hold them in; they bolted down the road, running away madly. I watched them out of sight, then looked for the stranger, but I found that he, too, was gone.

With a light heart I turned down the side road through the deepening valley to which Johann had objected. There was not the slightest reason, that I could see, for his objection; and I daresay I tramped for a couple of hours without thinking of time or distance, and certainly without seeing a person or a house. So far as the place was concerned, it was desolation itself. But I did not notice this particularly till, on turning a bend in the road, I came upon a scattered fringe of wood; then I recognised that I had been impressed unconsciously by the desolation of the region through which I had passed.

I sat down to rest myself, and began to look around. It struck me that it was considerably colder than it had been at the commencement of my walk—a sort of sighing sound seemed to be around me, with, now and then, high overhead, a sort of muffled roar. Looking upwards I noticed that great thick clouds were drifting rapidly across the sky from North to South at a great height. There were signs of coming storm in some lofty stratum of the air. I was a little chilly, and, thinking that it was the sitting still after the exercise of walking, I resumed my journey.

The ground I passed over was now much more picturesque. There were no striking objects that the eye might single out; but in all there was a charm of beauty. I took little heed of time and it was only when the deepening twilight forced itself upon me that I began to think of how I should find my way home. The brightness of the day had gone. The air was cold, and the drifting of clouds high overhead was more marked. They were accompanied by a sort of far-away rushing sound, through which seemed to come at intervals that mysterious cry which the driver had said came from a wolf. For a while I hesitated. I had said I would see the deserted village, so on I went, and presently came on a wide stretch of open country, shut in by hills all around. Their sides were covered with trees which spread down to the plain, dotting, in clumps, the gentler slopes and hollows which showed here and there. I followed with my eye the winding of the road, and saw that it curved close to one of the densest of these clumps and was lost behind it.

As I looked there came a cold shiver in the air, and the snow began to fall. I thought of the miles and miles of bleak country I had passed, and then hurried on to seek the shelter of the wood in front. Darker and darker grew the sky, and faster and heavier fell the snow, till the earth before and around me was a glistening white carpet the further edge of which was lost in misty vagueness. The road was here but crude, and when on the level its boundaries were not so marked, as when it passed through the cuttings; and in a little while I found that I must have strayed from it, for I missed underfoot the hard surface, and my feet sank deeper in the grass and moss. Then the wind grew stronger and blew with ever increasing force, till I was fain to run before it. The air became icy-cold, and in spite of my exercise I began to suffer. The snow was now falling so thickly and whirling around me in such rapid eddies that I could hardly keep my eyes open. Every now and then the heavens were torn asunder by vivid lightning, and in the flashes I could see ahead of me a great mass of trees, chiefly yew and cypress all heavily coated with snow.

I was soon amongst the shelter of the trees, and there, in comparative silence, I could hear the rush of the wind high overhead. Presently the blackness of the storm had become merged in the darkness of the night. By-and-by the storm seemed to be passing away: it now only came in fierce puffs or blasts. At such moments the weird sound of the wolf appeared to be echoed by many similar sounds around me.

Now and again, through the black mass of drifting cloud, came a straggling ray of moonlight, which lit up the expanse, and showed me that I was at the edge of a dense mass of cypress and yew trees. As the snow had ceased to fall, I walked out from the shelter and began to investigate more closely. It appeared to me that, amongst so many old foundations as I had passed, there might be still standing a house in which, though in ruins, I could find some sort of shelter for a while. As I skirted the edge of the copse, I found that a low wall encircled it, and following this I presently found an opening. Here the cypresses formed an alley leading up to a square mass of some kind of building. Just as I caught sight of this, however, the drifting clouds obscured the moon, and I passed up the path in darkness. The wind must have grown colder, for I felt myself shiver as I walked; but there was hope of shelter, and I groped my way blindly on.

I stopped, for there was a sudden stillness. The storm had passed; and, perhaps in sympathy with nature's silence, my heart seemed to cease to beat. But this was only momentarily; for suddenly the moonlight broke through the clouds, showing me that I was in a graveyard, and that the square object before me was a great massive tomb of marble, as white as the snow that lay on and all around it. With the moonlight there came a fierce sigh of the storm, which appeared to resume its course with a long, low howl, as of many dogs or wolves. I was awed and shocked, and felt the cold perceptibly grow upon me till it seemed to grip me by the heart. Then while the flood of moonlight still fell on the marble tomb, the storm gave further evidence of renewing, as though it was returning on its track. Impelled by some sort of fascination, I approached the sepulchre to see what it was, and why such a thing stood alone in such a place. I walked around it, and read, over the Doric door, in German:

COUNTESS DOLINGEN OF GRATZ
IN STYRIA
SOUGHT AND FOUND DEATH
1801

On the top of the tomb, seemingly driven through the solid marble—for the structure was composed of a few vast blocks of stone—was a great iron spike or stake. On going to the back I saw, graven in great Russian letters:

"The dead travel fast."

There was something so weird and uncanny about the whole thing that it gave me a turn and made me feel quite faint. I began to wish, for the first time, that I had taken Johann's advice. Here a thought struck me, which came under almost mysterious circumstances and with a terrible shock. This was Walpurgis Night!

Walpurgis Night, when, according to the belief of millions of people, the devil was abroad—when the graves were opened and the dead came forth and walked. When all evil things of earth and air and water held revel. This very place the driver had specially shunned. This was the depopulated village of centuries ago. This was where the suicide lay; and this was the place where I was alone—unmanned, shivering with cold in a shroud of snow with a wild storm gathering again upon me! It took all my philosophy, all the religion I had been taught, all my courage, not to collapse in a paroxysm of fright.

And now a perfect tornado burst upon me. The ground shook as though thousands of horses thundered across it; and this time the storm bore on its icy wings, not snow, but great hailstones which drove with such violence that they might have come from the thongs of Balearic slingers—hailstones that beat down leaf and branch and made the shelter of the cypresses of no more avail than though their stems were standing-corn. At the first I had rushed to the nearest tree; but I was soon fain to leave it and seek the only spot that seemed to afford refuge, the deep Doric doorway of the marble tomb. There, crouching against the massive bronze door, I gained a certain amount of protection from the beating of the hailstones, for now they only drove against me as they ricocheted from the ground and the side of the marble.

As I leaned against the door, it moved slightly and opened inwards. The shelter of even a tomb was welcome in that pitiless tempest, and I was about to enter it when there came a flash of forked-lightning that lit up the whole expanse of the heavens. In the instant, as I am a living man, I saw, as my eyes were turned into the darkness of the tomb, a beautiful woman, with rounded cheeks and red lips, seemingly sleeping on a bier. As the thunder broke overhead, I was grasped as by the hand of a giant and hurled out into the storm. The whole thing was so sudden that, before I could realise the shock, moral as well as physical, I found the hailstones beating me down. At the same time I had a strange, dominating feeling that I was not alone. I looked towards the tomb. Just then there came another blinding flash, which seemed to strike the iron stake that surmounted the tomb and to pour through to the earth, blasting and crumbling the marble, as in a burst of flame. The dead woman rose for a moment of agony, while she was lapped in the flame, and her bitter scream of pain was drowned in the thundercrash. The last thing I heard was this mingling of dreadful sound, as again I was seized in the giant-grasp and dragged away, while the hailstones beat on me, and the air around seemed reverberant with the howling of wolves. The last sight that I remembered was a vague, white, moving mass, as if all the graves around me had sent out the phantoms of their sheeted-dead, and that they were closing in on me through the white cloudiness of the driving hail.

Gradually there came a sort of vague beginning of consciousness; then a sense of weariness that was dreadful. For a time I remembered nothing; but slowly my senses returned. My feet seemed positively racked with pain, yet I could not move them. They seemed to be numbed. There was an icy feeling at the back of my neck and all down my spine, and my ears, like my feet, were dead, yet in torment; but there was in my breast a sense of warmth which was, by comparison, delicious. It was as a nightmare—a physical nightmare, if one may use such an expression; for some heavy weight on my chest made it difficult for me to breathe.

This period of semi-lethargy seemed to remain a long time, and as it faded away I must have slept or swooned. Then came a sort of loathing, like the first stage of sea-sickness, and a wild desire to be free from something—I knew not what. A vast stillness enveloped me, as though all the world were asleep or dead—only broken by the low panting as of some animal close to me. I felt a warm rasping at my throat, then came a consciousness of the awful truth, which chilled me to the heart and sent the blood surging up through my brain. Some great animal was lying on me and now licking my throat. I feared to stir, for some instinct of prudence bade me lie still; but the brute seemed to realise that there was now some change in me, for it raised its head. Through my eyelashes I saw above me the two great flaming eyes of a gigantic wolf. Its sharp white teeth gleamed in the gaping red mouth, and I could feel its hot breath fierce and acrid upon me.

For another spell of time I remembered no more. Then I became conscious of a low growl, followed by a yelp, renewed again and again. Then, seemingly very far away, I heard a "Holloa! holloa!" as of many voices calling in unison. Cautiously I raised my head and looked in the direction whence the sound came; but the cemetery blocked my view. The wolf still continued to yelp in a strange way, and a red glare began to move round the grove of cypresses, as though following the sound. As the voices drew closer, the wolf yelped faster and louder. I feared to make either sound or motion. Nearer came the red glow, over the white pall which stretched into the darkness around me. Then all at once from beyond the trees there came at a trot a troop of horsemen bearing torches. The wolf rose from my breast and made for the cemetery. I saw one of the horsemen (soldiers by their caps and their long military cloaks) raise his carbine and take aim. A companion knocked up his arm, and I heard the ball whizz over my head. He had evidently taken my body for that of the wolf. Another sighted the animal as it slunk away, and a shot followed. Then, at a gallop, the troop rode forward—some towards me, others following the wolf as it disappeared amongst the snow-clad cypresses.

As they drew nearer I tried to move, but was powerless, although I could see and hear all that went on around me. Two or three of the soldiers jumped from their horses and knelt beside me. One of them raised my head, and placed his hand over my heart.

"Good news, comrades!" he cried. "His heart still beats!"

Then some brandy was poured down my throat; it put vigour into me, and I was able to open my eyes fully and look around. Lights and shadows were moving among the trees, and I heard men call to one another. They drew together, uttering frightened exclamations; and the lights flashed as the others came pouring out of the cemetery pell-mell, like men possessed. When the further ones came close to us, those who were around me asked them eagerly:

"Well, have you found him?"

The reply rang out hurriedly:

"No! no! Come away quick—quick! This is no place to stay, and on this of all nights!"

"What was it?" was the question, asked in all manner of keys. The answer came variously and all indefinitely as though the men were moved by some common impulse to speak, yet were restrained by some common fear from giving their thoughts.

"It—it—indeed!" gibbered one, whose wits had plainly given out for the moment.

"A wolf—and yet not a wolf!" another put in shudderingly.

"No use trying for him without the sacred bullet," a third remarked in a more ordinary manner.

"Serve us right for coming out on this night! Truly we have earned our thousand marks!" were the ejaculations of a fourth.

"There was blood on the broken marble," another said after a pause—"the lightning never brought that there. And for him—is he safe? Look at his throat! See, comrades, the wolf has been lying on him and keeping his blood warm."

The officer looked at my throat and replied:

"He is all right; the skin is not pierced. What does it all mean? We should never have found him but for the yelping of the wolf."

"What became of it?" asked the man who was holding up my head, and who seemed the least panic-stricken of the party, for his hands were steady and without tremor. On his sleeve was the chevron of a petty officer.

"It went to its home," answered the man, whose long face was pallid, and who actually shook with terror as he glanced around him fearfully. "There are graves enough there in which it may lie. Come, comrades—come quickly! Let us leave this cursed spot."

The officer raised me to a sitting posture, as he uttered a word of command; then several men placed me upon a horse. He sprang to the saddle behind me, took me in his arms, gave the word to advance; and, turning our faces away from the cypresses, we rode away in swift, military order.

As yet my tongue refused its office, and I was perforce silent. I must have fallen asleep; for the next thing I remembered was finding myself standing up, supported by a soldier on each side of me. It was almost broad daylight, and to the north a red streak of sunlight was reflected, like a path of blood, over the waste of snow. The officer was telling the men to say nothing of what they had seen, except that they found an English stranger, guarded by a large dog.

"Dog! that was no dog," cut in the man who had exhibited such fear. "I think I know a wolf when I see one."

The young officer answered calmly: "I said a dog."

"Dog!" reiterated the other ironically. It was evident that his courage was rising with the sun; and, pointing to me, he said, "Look at his throat. Is that the work of a dog, master?"

Instinctively I raised my hand to my throat, and as I touched it I cried out in pain. The men crowded round to look, some stooping down from their saddles; and again there came the calm voice of the young officer:

"A dog, as I said. If aught else were said we should only be laughed at."

I was then mounted behind a trooper, and we rode on into the suburbs of Munich. Here we came across a stray carriage, into which I was lifted, and it was driven off to the Quatre Saisons— the young officer accompanying me, whilst a trooper followed with his horse, and the others rode off to their barracks.

When we arrived, Herr Delbrück rushed so quickly down the steps to meet me, that it was apparent he had been watching within. Taking me by both hands he solicitously led me in. The officer saluted me and was turning to withdraw, when I recognised his purpose, and insisted that he should come to my rooms. Over a glass of wine I warmly thanked him and his brave comrades for saving me. He replied simply that he was more than glad, and that Herr Delbrück had at the first taken steps to make all the searching party pleased; at which ambiguous utterance the maître d'hôtel smiled, while the officer pleaded duty and withdrew.

"But Herr Delbrück," I enquired, "how and why was it that the soldiers searched for me?"

He shrugged his shoulders, as if in depreciation of his own deed, as he replied:

"I was so fortunate as to obtain leave from the commander of the regiment in which I served, to ask for volunteers."

"But how did you know I was lost?" I asked.

"The driver came hither with the remains of his carriage, which had been upset when the horses ran away."

"But surely you would not send a search-party of soldiers merely on this account?"

"Oh, no!" he answered; "but even before the coachman arrived, I had this telegram from the Boyar whose guest you are," and he took from his pocket a telegram which he handed to me, and I read:

Bistritz.

> Be careful of my guest—his safety is most precious to me. Should aught happen to him, or if he be missed, spare nothing to find him and ensure his safety. He is English and therefore adventurous. There are often dangers from snow and wolves and night. Lose not a moment if you suspect harm to him. I answer your zeal with my fortune.—*Dracula.*

As I held the telegram in my hand, the room seemed to whirl around me; and, if the attentive maître d'hôtel had not caught me, I think I should have fallen. There was something so strange in all this, something so weird and impossible to imagine, that there grew on me a sense of my being in some way the sport of opposite forces—the mere vague idea of which seemed in a way to paralyse me. I was certainly under some form of mysterious protection. From a distant country had come, in the very nick of time, a message that took me out of the danger of the snow-sleep and the jaws of the wolf.

Dracula's Guest first appeared in the June 1914 issue of *The Story-Teller* under the title "Walpurgis Night." Later that year it became the title story in the collection *Dracula's Guest and Other Weird Tales*

Bram Stoker(1847-1912) was an Irish civil servant, theater manager, and writer. His most famous wok, *Dracula*, has become a classic of Gothic horror fiction and has inspired countless adaptations, sequels, and imitators.

LAST RITES

So Many Wives
By Holly Payne-Strange

<u>**The First—Wales, 973**</u>

He had never lived with anyone before
Although 'lived' was a relative term, of course.
He had hoped it would be easy with her, that she would sit pretti-
ly on his knee,
Like a doll
Or a napkin, stained at dinner time.

She was, after all, nothing but a peasant girl,
Barefoot and shy with smiles,
Never had a bath before.
Her figure and form the only real thing of note.
Surely, she should know how to behave, how to please.

Instead, it was just awkward.
She sat where he said and did as she was told,
But somehow they didn't quite fit, like a sword in the wrong
hand,
Or a cape on backwards.

He didn't realize it, but she was clever.
She gave him exactly what he thought he wanted,
But only an echo of what he really desired.
Docile as water
That carves a riverbed

Too slow for any to notice.

And so in this way, he left her alone,
Tiring of tepid attempts
And unobjecting apathy.

And as he went away, more and more,
She studied,
More and more.
Creeping into his library and stealing his precious books,
Soaking it up.
Waiting.

Even the shadows must beware a patient woman.
Her time would come.

So Many Wives

<u>The Second—Almohad Caliphate, 1162</u>

She had always been arrogant.
Her father hated her for it, claiming it was an affront to him, her
brother, and Allah.
Jewels that shine bright need the most 'protection'.
She didn't care.

So when a handsomish_stranger appeared one day
Claiming enough riches to embarrass a jinn
But clearly ill at ease on a camel
She was hardly impressed.

It seemed to infuriate the man, a fact she found incredibly funny.
And when he tried, pushed harder and harder to impress,
Making wild claims of blood and bats,
Of shape shifting and superhuman strength,
She just said, 'prove it' and led him to her father.
Neither of them hesitated a moment as he bled the man dry,
Rubies pooling at their feet.

She leapt on the stranger then, no hypnotism required.
That seemed to surprise the count, as if burned by the shock of
real passion,
Kisses like molten gold on bare skin.

It was only after they were done that she begged,
'Let me kill my brother,
And I will serve you
Till the end of the moon.'

She was an artist, carving up his body with patience, reverence.
Each drop of blood a song,
A show for her new
LoverMasterFriendFoeCaptorGuardian

They left her balmy shores, the Sahara, and the sun,
In exchange for somewhere colder, wetter, darker,
Where thunder reigned and the rain thundered,
Hammering against his
-Their-
Castle windows with a diamond ferocity.
And when she met The First, the two of them smiled.
It would be easier now.
They outnumbered him.

So Many Wives

The Third—Naples, 1712

My dearest Dracula,
I must apologize, but I am
Unavailable
To meet at Monday's masquerade.
I am afraid my sweet sister has rather ruined the surprise!
And I do not think I have time
For a blood soaked, bloodless demise,
Or a little light decapitation.

However.

It would be immensely impolite of me to leave a guest,
A stranger to our salubrious city,
Unfulfilled and unsatisfied.

I have the acquaintance of a certain Caterina Ricci, Contessa di
Firenze
-Disgraced, she won't be missed-
I'm sure she would scream
To sit and sup with such a successful suitor.
Do let me know if you would like me to make an introduction.

If this pleases you, I have a number of other
Friends
You may find fascinating.

Always happy
To be of service.

Signed,
XOXOXO

The Three—Transylvania, 1805

Sometimes He brought in Others.
A girl with an empire waistline,
And one who talked about engines and steam.
There was even a man once.
The wives could tell he wouldn't last long,
And they were completely correct,
His body soon dumped into the moat.

None of them lasted
Because none of them could run the gauntlet
Of the Sapphic Sisters.

They were vicious and nasty and really quite horrible.
But they were in love.
With each other, not with Him. He was a little irrelevant, really.
The First cared for the others, taking their hands and imposing
order.
The Third kissed them sweetly, licorice words and candy smiles,
Smoothing over even the worst of disagreements.

And the Second fought.
She screamed for what they deserved
And hounded Him even when the others shrank back.
She liked being the hero.

But they had stepped beyond life and death,
Beyond humanity and time.
So of course they hunted in packs,
Shirking silly expectations like monogamy and corsets.

They chased their prey with subtle sighs, and the roar of flowing
skirts.
And even He couldn't help but notice

So Many Wives

The giggling efficiency
With which they hunted.

So one day He said, "Sit here, on my lap, like a doll."

And in unison they said "No."

And that was that.
He never asked again.

Holly Payne-Strange is a novelist, poet and podcast creator. Her writing has been lauded by USA Today, LA weekly and The New York Times. She has had her poetry published by various groups including Door Is A Jar magazine, Icebreaker Lit, In Parenthesis, and Dipity Lit Magazine, among others.